SIDE
EFFECTS

– MYRNA BROWN –

FriesenPress

Suite 300 - 990 Fort St
Victoria, BC, V8V 3K2
Canada

www.friesenpress.com

Photography by Michal Lee
Edited by Robert Raleigh

ISBN
978-1-5255-0741-0 (Hardcover)
978-1-5255-0742-7 (Paperback)
978-1-5255-0743-4 (eBook)

1. FICTION, COMING OF AGE

Distributed to the trade by The Ingram Book Company

Twenty per cent of Americans have mental health issues. About 56% do not have access to care. After family doctors, psychiatrists are the most sought after physicians. Sophie's story can't possibly portray either the root cause of her behavior, or offer a remedy. It is simply one woman's journey through an acute onset of psychotic behavior. While it offers the reader an opportunity to see how Sophie's childhood may have affected her, and how she begins to heal, it offers no professional insight. It allows an opportunity for her story to be told.

To my husband and friend, Denis

Acknowledgments:

My friends: Terri Littlejohn, John and Eileen Ballance, Robert Raleigh, Inge and Volker Dube, Jim Hagen, Charlene Comtois, who bolster my confidence and contribute uniquely to my efforts.

My daughters: Michal Lee, Dana Shalom Ramsey who through loss and pain continue to encourage me.

SIDE
EFFECTS

– M Y R N A   B R O W N –

1974
Fremont, California

Sophie was lost, but she didn't know.
    She didn't know about psychotic breaks.
    She trusted her mind.
    It was a good mind; it excelled when she tried her best.
    Seated in front of her grandmother's walnut vanity, she felt the ends of her burned, auburn bangs.
    She cut them, and they made a nest in her hand, like a seared puff of pubic hair.
    She cut off more than the brittle ends,
    Whacking to the scalp the part that had caught fire,
    She was using the first pair of scissors she had come upon in the kitchen drawer, rusty and dull.

    Candles, including several red-ribboned, green bayberry, burned in the kitchen. All the candles in the house were lit. She had chosen sandal wood for the bedroom where she leaned into the mirror-winged, hand-me-down vanity. The odor was curdled by the acrid smell of singed hair. These scents, though pervasive, were soon mingled with the perfumes from other rooms. They tangled in the air, a mélange much like the inside of a store at the mall: sage, sea grass, vanilla, tropical night.
    The flame from the taper in the pewter candlestick had ignited her hair as she leaned in to light another. She had dabbed her forehead with a kitchen towel. The terry cloth was scorched, and some of her smoldering hair stuck

1

to it. She tossed it onto the white kitchen counter, pinching her nose because the smoke circling her face smelled just like the smell of a newly plucked and singed hen ready for the roasting pan, the kind her grandmother had often killed and prepared for their evening supper.

The doorbell rang. Sophie startled then peeked from the side of the blind. She saw her most nosy neighbor, Rosella, a woman of perhaps fifty-five or sixty, at the door. Her long gray hair was knotted as always at her neck. She came with a casserole. Repayment of sorts, Sophie supposed. Sophie had delivered several dishes to Rosella when she broke her leg.

Sophie hadn't been out of the house lately. Nosy Rosy must have noticed. Sophie didn't want to be interrupted. She didn't make a sound, and so the Corning Ware dish sat on the porch with the steam collecting under its glass lid until late in the day.

Before picking up the scissors again, Sophie examined the shriveled hair still clutched in her hand, no longer the soft, wispy curls she found hard to coif. Returning to the mirror, she cut more chunks off, not caring where they fell. Her salon style was ruined, but Sophie believed she looked better: more like the tomboy she'd grown up feeling herself to be. This new cut was something similar to Anna's baldness. She didn't really know why she cut it, except that it felt good. It felt final.

But Anna was dying of ovarian cancer. Maybe Anna would feel Sophie was fighting the disease with her. When you are losing someone, the resounding grief recurs like a malignancy, replicating itself throughout the body. There are no other useful metaphors. One gets through a valley. One climbs to the summit. One navigates the swelling seas. One fords the river. But in grief, there is no accomplishment to be made. One lives with the inevitability of its constancy. One resigns one's self to the guarantee of grief's presence, a presence that alters how the world is seen and experienced. Grief is permanent and not to be exploited for a lesson learned, not a journey that will end. The loss is for keeps, invasive and not to be matched by our wits or strength. Because we, too, are lost, we mourn ourselves. The actual face of death is wrenchingly sober and we can but distract ourselves. Although it was unclear to Sophie why she thought of her best friend as she cut her hair in defiance of her grief, she felt lighter as if Anna would have understood had she been there to witness the act.

Anna knew she could be impulsive. They were constantly returning shoes to the mall because Sophie wouldn't settle for uncomfortable or ugly shoes. There were few that satisfied her after impulsively buying them and toting them home. She never wore them out. She'd had her day with worn out shoes.

But this was more than normal impulsivity as she yanked up the hair and cut it off.

Now, when Sophie visited the hospital, Anna most often put her head back and closed her eyes. Sophie held her hand, sometimes all morning. She read Baudelaire in French, because Anna loved the music of the language.

Even though Anna had lived with her Norwegian mother and had gone back to the old country each summer, she hadn't learned her mother's native tongue. But having been exposed to many Scandinavian tongues, she found the mystery of foreign languages all the more exciting. Her father, Jack, died when she was a baby. Maybe if Anna had heard them speak together in the home, she might have been more receptive to it, she often said. As it was, she had simply acquired a slight accent. The sound of Anna's voice always stirred Sophie, like a call to be back with the sky below, in her childhood swing dreaming of becoming somebody, someone free and following the path of one of her fantasies.

The ropes had begun to shred where she held on the tightest, pumping her way until she saw that sky below her feet, going higher still. In the moment before the vanity, not realizing the depth of her break, her responsibility for her brothers brought her back. She imagined skidding her feet along the grass to stop, wondering, wondering, *how had it happened?* Before, she could promise something to get them to push her higher. Forever after, her promises to them would damn her.

Sophie looked in the mirror once more wondering if she were attractive enough for Steve. If not Steve, someone else might give her space enough to be truly herself. Fantasies played in her head, and the freshly gutted feeling of losing Anna was less visceral.

Who is the richer, the one who plays unguarded fantasies through her mind, fleshing out and expanding upon her dreams, or the one who aborts each foray that might actually induce intrusive, morally dubious, though admittedly compelling thoughts? Sophie's mind bled with unrestrained fantastical and confused thoughts.

Sophie's original dream was all but expired, and she had begun to displace her longings by want of a religious experience that might meet the starving need that repeated penitence had never afforded. It was an absence of joy. Sophie wanted to know God, as others claimed they did. She wanted a miracle, but the deaf ear of God made her mind go mad. She needed forgiveness. Just a nod. She needed healing for Anna. Just a touch.

Sophie's dark, dilated eyes looked back at her as she clipped hair off the back, even the part she couldn't see for good measure. The coppery curls fell like feathers, settling gently into *c*-shapes on the floor.

The scissors left a rusty scuff mark on the dresser scarf. She wet her finger to rub it off, but the stain spread wider and deeper into the white tatting. She stood and picked up the hand-worked dresser scarf her grandmother had given her. Before she died, she had allowed Marie, Sophie's older sister, to choose which of the linens she wanted. When Sophie chose from what was left, she was happy to get this particular one - the most delicate and complicated to stitch.

Now she carefully cut away the rusty spot, keeping fabric and blade close to her face for precision. She smoothed the damaged piece back onto the vanity, deeply satisfied she had fixed it.

Sophie hadn't slept. The praying and fasting had lasted four days. Yes, she was praying to have a tangible experience with God, the Father, or Whoever was available, someone who could help her atone and heal. She had hoped against hope that she might have an "in" with God and could maybe twist His arm if she ever got through. Some kind of relief was needed. There was no other resource, not even in her anticipatory deranged thinking.

She prayed for her best friend Anna, who was too young to die, but God remained a stranger, an island she could never seem to row to ... But Sophie would swim if she had to. She would trudge the golden shores to be received and blessed.

Her stomach gurgled as she bent prayerfully, head in her hands, amongst the many recently purchased and fiercely burning candles and read from her personal Bible; She was doing all she knew to do. She tarried. She knelt. She stood. She walked the dark hallway.

On the counter she saw the Sperry & Hutchison stamps. She was tempted to paste the green trading stamps in her book: she was saving for the Oneida stainless steel flatware set. But she returned to seeking God, shelving the idea as a selfish thought.

She allowed herself a half-glass of water every four hours. When she nodded asleep in the chair, she caught herself, wanting always to be awake and praying, just as Jesus had asked of His disciples the night before he was hung on the cross to die for the sins of all who came to Him.

Over the past four days she had committed all her time to her plea to God. Steve, her husband, hadn't noticed, even though she was pale and her hands had trembled yesterday when she served him a limp salad with a hamburger patty and a baked potato for dinner, a far cry from the pepper steak with a flare of cognac she prepared on a good day. When she tried a Béarnaise sauce for filet mignon it failed. But still she pursued Julia Child's cavalier attitude toward food. She could scoot an omelet out of its pan, and it would slide oozing its cheese into the center of the plate.

She continued to deny herself baked potatoes or any of her favorites. She rubbed the spuds in butter before she baked them, and their skins went crispy. She could almost taste the salty, melted butter, watch it saturating the mealy potato as she incised the skin.

He had eaten by himself in the kitchen without complaint, not questioning why she wasn't eating or why she hadn't gone to the store. After all, she was often on a restrictive diet to keep her figure.

He read *The Fremont Times* she had folded next to his plate. Her name was in a back section which featured those students who had excelled at the Ohlone Community College. He hadn't noticed, distracted by an article about drug use and the remarkable turn-around among addicts at meetings being held at the American Legion Hall.

Their evenings together were few, what with the activities of a youth pastor. He was trying to get the business of being a minister down pat. During their time at the theological seminary in Denver, she had worked as a teller at Columbia Savings and Loan for barely enough to get by. Now he wants children, but she hasn't accomplished her elusive dream to do lectures on Shakespeare, Austen, Conrad or Dickens, let alone write. She wondered about the legitimacy of her quest. The book *Heart of Darkness* lay in her mind like a hot coal. Is man ultimately evil?

5

People had come into the bank with their savings passes to be updated. They generally looked poor coming in, and she would be astounded at their large balances. She was poor but wanted very much to look stylish. She was without much of a wardrobe. Still it was selfish of her to want to be spiffy and coordinated.

She had spent grocery money on something she took a liking to, like the light wool dress. Steve had held it up and said "You spent that much on this?"

Fortunately, the bank provided the tellers uniforms, suits of wool by Hart Schaffner & Marx. She had church clothes, but they were going out of style.

Beyond their means. Everything was beyond their means back then. They couldn't have paid for her to go to school at the same time. His vocation took priority, they had agreed.

Ten years into the marriage, at twenty-nine, Sophie understood she was not spiritual enough or formally educated enough to be his equal. They had stayed long enough at seminary for him to earn his doctorate. They moved often after leaving Denver, at the beck and call of the Baptist administration. More and more of his time became taken up outside their life together.

Steve talked to her of children as if it were her obligation. He wanted a family before it was too late. His mother, Alice, had spoken to him alone more than once. Sophie stayed on the pill. She didn't feel ready and had mixed feelings about having a baby. Maybe she didn't see Steve as the fathering type.

He was certainly very different from her father. Steve was rarely stirred to anger or joviality. She sensed his condescension. His emotions had always been in check, until finally it seemed he had none; only an aspiration to succeed in what he called "his life's work".

Teen Challenge ... founded in Oakland just up the Nimitz freeway from Fremont, California where they were sent ... had been organized with a single mission: to save addicts and take them off the streets. Steve was assigned by the senior pastor to support the growing organization that was renowned in churches across the entire East Bay area.

The crowd had become large, partly owing to his hard work. He spent hours with young men, sometimes women, talking them into coming to the mission and off the streets, out of their communes and ghettos, luring them to salvation and away from their world of addiction and drunkenness. Heroin and cocaine were boundless among the young users he said; old needles lay about, and many were picked up and reused. It epitomized spreading the Gospel to the least of them. They were immersed even as they held the pills in their fists.

The inter-denominational rallies Steve oversaw were held twice weekly, but the strung-out addicts collected on the premises throughout the day like bums on Seattle's waterfront Skid Row he said. They ate the meals the women's circle had prepared and wore the coats they provided. Sophie was not often invited. It was no place for her, Steve explained. He didn't even want her to go with him to the rallies.

"It's a rough crowd," he said. "You're not strong enough in the Lord."

She didn't want to attend the rallies. She knew very well she didn't belong. *Strong enough?* How could he measure her spirituality? She would be like Christ then: the only model of God on earth she and the world knew. So she had embarked on her personal journey to imitate Jesus. She would be good enough and strong enough to work alongside Steve. She would *make* herself want this life.

Steve, now well known among the congregation, sat prestigiously in the sanctuary on Sunday mornings behind the senior pastor. Reserved, he didn't raise his hands in worship like the others, but closed his eyes, bent over with his hands clasped in front of him, and bowing his head as if in grave meditation and prayer. He was dignified in all his ways.

He sang the choruses from memory. "*Standing somewhere in the shadows, you'll find Jesus. He's the One who always cares and understands, and you'll know Him by the nail prints in His hands.* "He was a tenor and even though he was bent at the waist his voice carried through the modern sound system in deep, clear notes.

Sophie had matriculated into many schools during the period of their marriage especially into Junior Colleges where she could get the required courses out of the way early mornings or late evenings, when they would not disrupt her housekeeping duties. She had spent a great deal of time in classrooms with much younger students. She was a late bloomer.

When she met one of her professors for coffee a second time, she recorded in her diary that she felt an intellectual attraction toward him due to his expertise at pulling the meaning out of a poem or story. It was almost like being inside the author's head, she marveled. The anatomy of a poem took on flesh.

Steve was against her educational bent and resented that she had given the professor her time outside the class room. After reading her diary, Steve had informed her: "You can't have secrets from me," and he tore out the offending pages, ripping them up and letting the shreds fall to the floor.

Shamefully, she gathered them up and dumped the papers, diary and all, into the bin where the wet coffee grounds pebbled and stained them. What right did she have to write her private thoughts, after all?

She had started again and had begun to hide them. Was it wrong to have private thoughts and desires? She had given away her privacy by being careless and too trusting, lessons she should have learned in her childhood. That day in the moment of her mind's chaotic turn, she dug the subsequent entries out of her personal trunk of keepsakes and ripped them up.

Fleetingly, she thought of the burn barrel of her childhood. Surely it was a sin to hide thoughts and deeds. She would be truthful and transparent, if only she could sense His presence.

If being close to God was attainable, she wanted the whole of it, the gut changing feelings that should come with an epiphany and close fellowship. In her life she hadn't found spiritual acceptance and peace, some kind of forgiveness for her misdeeds. Within herself, she seemed immune to the Holy Spirit's presence and promptings. Why was she incapable of feeling acceptance? Clearly, she hadn't tried hard enough.

★★★

What did it mean to be descended upon like the day of Pentecost? Why did they have to wait fifty days in the Upper Room? She hoped for something to transform her, like Paul on the road to Damascus. He was lucky. That's right, she corrected herself, *there's no such thing as luck*. Everything was preordained. But prayer changes things, they also taught in contradiction.

The Sunday morning services in their new church, the pulsing heart of the sweeping evangelical movement, were different than any she had experienced before. The words of the songs flashed up on a screen, scrolling down as they sang; the hymnals were rarely used, and in abandoning them, the worshippers were more spontaneous and creative in their praises. More vigorous and demonstrative. The singing and the testimonies took up the space of an hour. Mostly, they stood, applauding, singing and praising the Lord.

The gold script was still legible on the unused brown hymnals spaced evenly in the rack. She leafed through, remarking on the strange metaphors: Nothing but the blood of Jesus could make you whiter than the snow.

She sat alone in the second row on the end. The beautiful wood of the pews reminded her of her father. The loss of the closeness they had had when she was a child … that loss was piercing. Being with him had satisfied her like nothing else in her entire life. He had protected her, comforted her wordlessly; he had been a presence to her. Near him her worries subsided even though she sinned against him almost daily. She had compromised her own integrity to get along. Now she knew that he had known when she made up stories just to get along.

The fleshy soprano with a welcoming bosom led the choir. Presiding, she turned to the congregation, and waved to them with both hands to stand and sing. She belted out the words, and her chest swelled even larger; the church vibrated. The lady's buttocks swayed to the music within the tight girdle like something upholstered. Sophie thought she was the main attraction, not Jesus or God, or the Holy Ghost.

Lisa, the young pianist, seemed under her spell and intuited when to change chords or simply play those altar-calling gospel songs of times past. She kept her eyes on the woman. Lisa held her hands above the keys, waiting for the next Spirit-led song.

Sophie didn't allow herself to raise her hands and sing like the others. She watched the wattle under the singer's chin as it quivered when she held a high note. Between songs, Sophie looked to the floor wondering what would come next.

"Let the Holy Spirit flow," the song leader, said holding the microphone close to her mouth, as she whispered against the static.

"Praise God, praise God." The sound of the 'p' pushed through the microphone as if she were spitting. She moved across the platform. She leaned into the audience. Sophie thought she was the main attraction, not Jesus or God or the Trinity, as one might say.

The minister stood, praising the song leader. He said, "Praise Jesus! One of Shirley's compositions that has led many a congregation and radio-TV audience to the very throne of God is 'His Name is Wonderful.' Oh, how she lifts believers and sin-sick hearts alike in adoration of the Lord with her majestic musical melodies and words! Teach it to us now, Shirley if you will."

She sang the new song through, solo. They followed her the next time, and the next until they knew it. Many were in tears, hands extended toward heaven.

"His name is wonderful / His name is wonderful, / Jesus, my Lord.

He's the great shepherd, / The rock of all ages, / Almighty God is He. Bow down before Him, / Love and adore Him, / His name is wonderful/ Jesus my Lord."

During the campaign Aubrey composed and taught many new songs of worship. The best remembered are: "I'll never be lonely again," "All He Wants

Is You," "He Belongs to Me," "It Matters to Him About You," "To Be Used of God" and "When You Pray."

The lines evoked an intimacy with God still a mystery to Sophie though it sounded as if it would be a walk in the garden if she could just imagine such a place.

Sophie watched Steve, noting his reaction to this charismatic woman who could bring people to tears. "The Holy Ghost" is visiting us, folks" she said. Steve bowed his head once more.

Sophie prayed that whatever it took she would be visited upon by the Holy Spirit. Like blind Bartimaeus, she wanted the scales to lift from her eyes to see objects she had only felt. But while others claimed Jesus as their personal savior and personal friend, she remained in the dark. He had rent the veil in two, admitting those seeking redemption. When would she feel she had passed through the veil into His Holy of Holies?

While Shirley continued to dominate the service, the congregants turned toward each other hugging and crying. A circle formed from which many hands came to rest on a sobbing woman's back. Clearly she was being moved by the Spirit. Some even talked in tongues, though in her mind, words had little to do with the relationship she craved.

Sophie didn't understand and didn't join in. Perhaps she would not be chosen as one of His followers. She hadn't even made initial contact. She couldn't be anything but honest with herself, and she felt simply alone and exiled. Her soul was a pit.

She tried raising her hands in praise wanting to be enthralled like the others, but the thrill of His presence didn't come. So many years, and it had never come.

Maybe it should be enough to shrug your spiritual-seeking shoulders and accept that you cannot know. But, just following along, was no longer working for Sophie. Her needs were deep, and she wanted to feel the closeness to God that others talked of, to be strong in the Lord, as Steve deemed she was not. Approval was hard to come by.

★★★

On this day ... the fourth day without food or sleep ... home alone, deep in prayer, stretched toward the imaginary light, out of her mind, she felt an urgency to share herself with someone as spiritual as she felt herself becoming. She wanted to be authenticated.

She called the senior pastor, but the secretary wouldn't put her through. She tried several times. The secretary gave reasons, but after three calls, she was dismissed altogether. He had appointments. Didn't the secretary hear the distress in her voice?

But, being dismissed by the secretary didn't mean she felt dismissed by God. *"No,"* she thought.

She would hound Him until she felt a significant change. She felt so close to a breakthrough. She replaced the receiver and sat with her hands folded in her lap. Even though it had been four days since she'd slept, she felt full of energy and expectation. Finally the hair her mother found so troublesome was taken care of, she thought proudly. To succeed in not being vain was an excellent step forward.

Soon she would sense the affirmation of Anna's healing. Anna, her best friend in every sense, would be with her again on the ski slopes in Tahoe, hardy and red-cheeked. With their matching purple mittens they would have another season of chatter and playfulness. They sometimes looked like twins by the choices they made in shoes and clothes, mostly thanks to Sophie's imitations of Anna, though not always.

Anna bought a single pearl necklace that fell just between the mounds of her modest breasts, just like Sophie's, whose pearl was given to her one Christmas by her brothers many years before.

Anna had never known her father except as a baby. She wore it in memory of him, just as Sophie wore hers in memory of her lost ones. Sophie and Anna were very different in ways but alike in many others.

Even their bra size was the same. In high school Anna had lent Sophie a safety pin when the strap of her worn bra broke. They kept extra tampons in their purses for each other. Their menstrual cycles often happened at the same time. Anna had curves, however, and Sophie had none.

"Straight as a stick," her brothers had teased. "You're no girl; girls don't play trucks and cars."

They had been in the shade of the large cedar from where her swing hung. The tire swing the boys favored had been hung on the edge of the forest from where they launched onto branches like Tarzan.

Strong friendship had come rarely to Sophie. Magically, it happened to both Anna and Sophie in the same moment. From their first meeting, Sophie had tended to her friendship with Anna as one would with a tidy, gated garden that been in disuse ... crumbling fine the dirt with gloveless hands, sorting out the tiniest pebbles, enriching the soil, keeping it moist. Like a garden, their friendship blossomed very simply and with few words spoken between them. The rested ground was fallow.

All through grade school, Sophie handled Anna's hair often, braiding the silky ashen strands almost reverently. Their oaths held in adolescence. How was it they could sit as teens together on a dock overhanging Lake Berryessa, their toes skimming the water, not touching, but living a wordless poem that unfolded in pure silence?

In friendship there is no dichotomy between the natural and the spiritual. They were comfortable together naked in the locker room or in the shower. They talked easily. They had sworn secrets.

As girls, they pranced like fillies in the open meadow beyond the football field, pretending they were trotting in a parade or pawing the grass. They snorted and whinnied. They loped and raced each other. There were no boys who mocked them. Sometimes just for fun, the first and second grade boys circled them, corralling them. Mostly they played alone, trotting in cadence, a little like the jogging they did as adults.

They wrote plays. Sophie took Anna to secret places in the woods where they acted them out, but there were places she couldn't bear to go after the tragedy. Anna was curious, but Sophie didn't talk of it. Anna knew the story when it swirled through the small community.

Sophie knew the rawness of loss. She had observed her mother, and cried when she cried. Ben, her father, cried silently. In spite of her own sorrow, Sophie played together with Anna. They could sit, hands folded like sophisticated ladies in grand chairs on the velour of mossy fallen trunks. They spread their pretend skirts and adjusted their veils. They read aloud together. They loved *Little Women*. Oh, to love and be loved the way that family loved each other. They were happy.

Sophie and Anna had talked easily, even after their marriages necessitated talking by phone. When Brett was transferred to the San Francisco Airport, neither could believe they would be almost neighbors. As a pilot, he was often away for several days at a time, and they would talk together long into the darkness.

Anna wanted a baby.

But now Anna is sick and has no hair. She is emaciated. Before she was diagnosed, though she didn't have her period, she ached in a different way constantly. She told Sophie it wasn't cramping she felt, but a deep pelvic pain, and she had a swollen, achy abdomen.

Brett can't be consoled, and Steve hadn't reached out to him. Steve was busy, importantly busy.

As was her nature, Sophie wanted both to comfort and be of help when visiting Anna, but not be in the way. "Oh, excuse me," Sophie would say during a visit when the nurse came to check Anna's IV line.

"Oh, I'm sorry," she said when someone came to take Anna's vitals. She might be in the way, but she wanted to be by Anna's side. Anna wanted her there and held her hand more tightly whenever she was washed over by a wave of pain. Sophie would go to the nurse's station to call the nurse. Sophie refreshed Anna's ice. The nurse would up the dose, and the drops of the IV bumped and bulged before they slid into her arm.

Anna would fall asleep, but Sophie stayed often and got into rush hour traffic on her way home. Steve would wonder about dinner.

As friends and neighbors, Anna and Sophie had jogged in the early mornings. That was the one part of their move from Oregon to Fremont that Sophie loved: they had settled in the same neighborhood as Anna and Brett. Fremont was a bedroom city: people could still afford to live there and accepted their long congested commutes to work. Brett had to cross the Bay Bridge for work. Most importantly, Fremont was near Steve's work.

Drying the backs of their necks, stepping in place to cool down, they would drink Fresca or Diet Coke on the patio or honeysuckle tea near the feeble flame of the ersatz logs. The goal was to keep their figures, and they succeeded. Being thin and tall, Sophie looked chic, Anna said, even though the curves were absent.

Sophie didn't often speak of Steve, but Anna nearly always had an interesting story that reflected her closeness with Brett, like biking around the lake in Fremont. They carried a blanket and lay in the grass together, watching the children play and wondering when it might happen for them. Anna didn't tell Brett about her pain until it was too late.

Brett even helped her tease her hair for a special event, before she lost it, that is: puffing it high into a heap in the back. He slid the comb gently through it and looped it into curls which he sprayed and rearranged and sprayed with All-net again.

Sophie had stopped trying to control her own curls.

Steve would never have helped with the giant rollers it took to straighten her hair. But no matter what she did, her hair was curly atop her head by the end of the day anyway. Her mother had hated dealing with her curls.

"She has a lot of it, but it's so fine, I can't manage it," Dorothy, her mother, informed everybody, it seemed. "Marie's hair goes right into ringlets," she would say, referring to Sophie's older sister.

As she continued to cut away at her hair, Sophie felt the old closeness to Anna. Sophie cut more away from around her ears and then off the top. She felt the rough patches, pleased. In her mind, she was sacrificing her hair for Anna. Somewhere inside, she wanted to go on the path Anna was on.

Her mind turned to her own vanity, the prideful attention she paid to herself. She should remove her "L'Aire du Temps" perfume.

She showered again, scrubbing her neck and wrists to remove any of the offending odors. Yes, Sophie believed she had finally prioritized her relationship with God. Had she not gone through a desert experience like John, the Baptist, without food, without sleep?

She soaped up the mound of coppery pubic hair and shaved it clean. As the hair flowed down the drain, she felt the coarseness of her pubic mound.

Anna was a friend for life; but her life would soon be over. Her cancer was at stage four: terminal. With Anna, Sophie had gotten a longed-for friendship ... one she'd pined for all her young life. Now she would lose that treasure.

And what would she have left? No one could fill the vacuum if she lost Anna. Must she be willing in God's eyes to let her go? Was Anna a like Jacob, a prize she must willingly offer if God so desired? Would God really require that she be willing before He acknowledged and blessed her, and let Anna live? What was it to Him if He gave them a miracle?

But Sophie didn't entertain or succumb to anger. She diverted her anger, even toward God.

As pre-teens and later, Sophie would take pride in the way Anna looked. "Which of these should I wear?" Anna would ask Sophie.

"The pleated one that shows off your waist."

"The pleats aren't pressed very well."

"I'll do them while you work on your hair. Here, let me have it." Sophie said.

She used a steam cloth on the very light wool dress, using straight pins to set the pleats along their original line.

She remembered now how the dress emphasized Anna's shape, how it swung and showed its colors gracefully when she turned.

Out of the shower, Sophie began to cry. She began to cry, not in sobs, but softly in a guttural moaning as she remembered Anna's hair in her hands, smooth and almost elastic at once. She had stroked it as she brushed it and Anna would throw her head back. Theirs was an intimacy that she would never find again, she just knew it.

The reveries about Anna may have continued had Sophie's mania not intensified. That fourth day and final day of her fast, Sophie looked at her polished pink nails and again saw her concession to vanity and pride. She found the clippers and cut them, unevenly and almost to the quick. She recalled how perfect her sister's doll had been. She recoiled from the memory, from its template representation of how a girl should look. She had made herself into something of a doll.

Why hadn't she realized it was her proud nature that had been in the way? She had become vain like her sister Marie.

She scrubbed off the polish. The lunar shapes of her toenail clippings remained on the floor like sprinkles of tiny fallen apple blossoms, and the bruised cotton balls looked like pink-tinged thistles along a country road back home.

She cut her small toenail too closely, nipping off the end of her toe, and the blood dropped onto the white linoleum floor of the bathroom. Fascinated, she knelt and drew small circles around a single drop, like the earth rotating around the sun. When she walked to the kitchen one could see the crimson imprints as the open wound stained the path in the carpet, already flattened by walking back and forth nearly all day.

After four days, she opened the refrigerator to cater to her own body's needs. She felt now as though she had done all she could do to communicate with this unresponsive Eternal Being, the three in one. The nearly-full bottle of orange juice fascinated her, and she turned it in the light.

Sophie broke her fast by drinking it. She drank a full glass. It so satisfied her that she drank another. The sweetness infused her blood; she experienced a rapturous relief from her need to beg God. The room was filled with bright light.

Standing near the patio doors, she opened the neck of her shirt to catch the afternoon warmth, tearing away the pearl as she did so, so that it fell with its gold chain curled about it into the pot of ivy near the sliding glass doors. She would never find it, nor did she ever replace it. It was irreplaceable. It was lost.

All of a sudden, it seemed right to be naked. The buttons of her blouse scattered into the corners as she tore it straight from her body. She pranced in the sunlight in the kitchen, glorying at having touched the hem of His garment. She ran both hands down her straight body. She was not crazy to her own reckoning. She felt her spirit break through her thick curtain of isolation.

Her racing mind was brilliant ... alive ... in touch with God! Anna would live. She was sure of it. Steve would sit with her in the evenings while they read; they would be quiet and close like a real couple. His work would become her work. She'd have his blessing and approval.

Even her sex life would change. They would have intercourse, and he would hold her those moments after when she quietly wanted more than she had received, not knowing how to ask, thinking the release should come about naturally the next time he penetrated her, though it never did.

She felt left behind, like something was wrong with her. She'd never had a lover and remained solely responsible for her own orgasms after she married. Steve didn't learn, and she didn't teach him.

Dougie, her brother would come to mind, and she sometimes remembered the misguided but sincere tenderness with which he approached her the first time. Also, Dougie would ride her on his shoulders when no one else was around, careful to hold her ankles as he went in circles. "Whoa, Boy," She'd said, grabbing a fistful of dark hair.

Her thoughts washed in quickly like a boat's wake against a buoy. Yes, everything would change! Anna would live. She would *want* to be submissive to Steve. She would put her heart into it. She'd stop expecting so much from him. His work was important, more important than her happiness. She wouldn't depend on his affections or anticipate his praise. She would do more to deserve it.

★★★

Sometime later the phone in the bedroom rang. She ran to it and put it under the bed. It rang and rang. She didn't answer. She wanted the ecstasy of this moment. The ring was threatening, a sign that something could interfere.

Now was a good time to let the Bible open where it might. Steve's Bible was on the nightstand. Surely she would be led to read a passage that would have even greater meaning for her in her changed state. She was on the threshold. She lay on her bed. Steve's Bible, the black leather King James with its binding cracked by use, fell open to the New Testament. She read "If we ask anything according to His will, He hears us …"

It was as if heaven had opened. Only believe! All things are possible, one just has to believe. She asked for Anna to live. She asked for Him to be her personal Savior, to give her the feelings she couldn't achieve on her own.

Her heart beat frantically in the recurring rhythm of a jungle drum. She had trouble breathing. Seeking God can make you go mad, and she was lost, unbeknownst to herself.

The blood from the cut on her small left toe seeped into the quilted bedspread, absorbed by the stitching. It made a fascinating arc as she turned, and she drew others below it with her toe, smudging the blood into the matelassé pattern, to form a rainbow: a beautiful rosy rainbow, like the color-saturated promise one sees in the mix of sunlight and rain. She imagined red raindrops sliding silently down the stems of leaves … channeling in the grooves of the leaves, in contrast to the greenness. They would bleed together on the porch railing and then evaporate just as if it had never rained at all. She knelt atop the bed over the simulated rainbow, (a strobe across her raw nerves), and she felt it and marveled at it as if it marked a new beginning.

Because the Bible fell open just past Third John to Revelations, Sophie began her discoveries in regards to becoming the Bride of Christ. No one could come any closer to the Father than that.

The hidden phone rang. She put a pillow over it under the bed. Muffled, it still rang, interrupting her thinking. Her thoughts scurried like rats in many different directions.

Sophie returned to the scriptures. She had never known she was *chosen*. How special she was to be someone of account, even *called*. If Christ saw her as a pure, submissive virgin, baptized symbolically in his purifying fountain and ready to meet Him, then surely, she, too, could celebrate as a soon-to-be bride might before the bedroom mirror, lifting her breasts carefully, strumming the nipples until they hardened, smoothing her cheeks with both hands, turning to see her profile, anticipating refinement by the fire of the Holy Spirit. Her pride and her doubts would be immolated. She would feel the embrace of her soul by the Father Himself.

After examining herself from head to toe, she took a small hand-held mirror with her, and she lay again on the rumpled bed reopening the Bible. She smiled into the reflection of oblivion, believing she saw herself transformed. She kissed the mirror. The fog of her breath bloomed and withered on its face.

She turned and laid the open Bible over her bare chest, and held the mirror closely as she looked into her own widened, wondering eyes. She smiled. She scowled. She lifted her one eyebrow. She stuck out her tongue. Her mouth was still dry; she allowed herself sips of water and went back to looking at the reflection of her face, realizing she would never really see it except in a mirror. She could see her hands, her arms, but there were parts of herself she would never see, her vagina, for example.

She took the mirror and knelt on the bed and unfolded the lush plumped lips of her vagina with the tips of her fingers. She moved the mirror and searched herself to see what had always before been hidden in darkness. She saw the varying shades of pink and red and marveled at the beauty. *Like an opening rose*, she thought as she pressed the petals further open. Beautiful to see, with a delightfully scented moisture, and her clitoris fully hardened like a bud. This seemed important to her.

Were there aspects of her she could not know? Had her soul been in darkness, had it ever really been seen or examined? Maybe, it too had this kind of fascinating beauty, which had never before seen the light? Was there more to her than she knew? Who would ever appreciate this beauty? Certainly not Steve, not even Anna. She alone could see it. Reverently she slipped her finger into the narrow cavity. She arched her back. She moved against her hand. She mewled when the explosion of pleasure came.

Brushing her arm against the spread, she was diverted by the sting of pain on her wrist, a burn from touching the rack of the oven. The scab had formed and hardened. She pulled the scab. The wound was deeper than she realized and it oozed. She put it to her mouth to ease the pain, tasting its saltiness. She pulled off the encrusted edges, too, and it began to bleed freely. Steve had suggested that if she left it alone, it would heal. But she habitually picked at the edges of her scabs as soon as they whitened.

The phone sounded plaintive as it rang again beneath the pillow under the bed. She squeezed the clip on the end of the cord, pulling it and letting the end drop. She lifted the phone back in its place on the bedside table.

Her whole body seemed dry. She found the blue jar of Noxzema. Much of its rich creaminess couldn't be absorbed. On her hand the lotion pulled into it the light and appeared iridescent like the scales of a deep-water fish. Its pungent, medical smell cooled her nostrils as she inhaled, and it was almost as if she tasted its tanginess. Her wrist stung. Noxzema was the wrong thing for an open sore.

As she slathered the cool lotion on her arms and legs, some soaked into the bed spread. The annoying toe continued to bleed. Finding a Band Aid in a bathroom drawer, she tried applying it, but the Noxzema on her hands interfered. She sat holding the corner of the bed skirt against her toe while holding the mirror, scowling to see how her face was affected in anger. She couldn't remember the last time she'd expressed anger, maybe as a child. People often remarked that she was sweet. She was known for her smile since childhood.

She noticed her right eyebrow was scorched. Inspired, wanting symmetry, she jumped to the bathroom to retrieve her husband's straight edged razor and scraped off the remaining brow. The burned skin of her forehead was bright red and tender to touch, but she completed the job.

She felt the ball of her foot touch the blood from her toe, and she knelt to examine the perfect outline of her foot, admiring how it arched and left a space upon the fake tile. She swiped at it with a white bath towel which

When Steve found her, he wrapped her in the bed sheet. He had been an orderly while doing his undergrad and had learned early how to restrain a patient. The mirror dropped from Sophie's hand. Cracks shot across its oval face, and it lay on the floor reflecting the ceiling plaster.

In that moment, her husband seemed like the Devil himself interrupting her reverie. She repeated the name of Jesus over and over.

"I'm the Bride of Christ; I just discovered I've been chosen by the Father," she said. "You should see. My vagina is beautiful. It folds out of itself like the petals of a rose."

The Bible was a safe piece of literature and she had begun to take to it. Now she believed she was clearly on the threshold of a newly found faith, really in touch with God. She pulled loose her arms. In garbled words between short, gasping breaths, she grasped at the Bible in spite of his forceful embrace. She wanted to show him the parts that had affected her, and flipped diligently through it leaving greasy fingerprints on the pages. Didn't he realize she was having a revelation of her own? God was visiting her

Steve was stunned to find his wife naked and incoherent, the house in utter disarray. In his confusion and anguish, seeing her naked aroused him. The curls where he smothered his face during their lovemaking were gone, and he knew he wouldn't experience her like that again, nor even touch the soft springiness of her curls.

He was fully and shamefully aroused as he wrapped the sheet across her smooth belly, keeping her arms next to her body. Why amidst this crisis was his desire so potent? Dismissing the question, he reached with his free hand and exposed himself. He felt a wrenching loss and shame as he ejaculated against the sheet around her belly. He would never recover from that shame, or from believing he was at least a part of what had caused his wife's breakdown.

But she had always just tagged along. She was so submissive and willing to let him lead. It had become his habit to scold her and she never angered. What had changed?

Sophie cried out and fell backward, unable to right herself. He held her as if a dance had ended. She swayed forward and he felt the weight of her against his arms as she found her balance.

Afterwards, when he had calmed in the wake of his orgasm, he asked her, "Why are you trying to look like Anna?"

Sophie felt his use of Anna's name was in vain. How could he know the importance of Anna's friendship when he had nothing like it in his life? He didn't seem to need friends, perhaps his mother, Alice, but not friends.

Sophie thrashed against him once more.

"Sophie," he meant to call her out of her state.

She looked sternly back at him, her eyes not leaving his face. She scowled the eerie scowl she had practiced in the mirror. It felt good to be angry.

Careful to keep her wrapped, he lay her down, not saying her name, not brushing her brow or smoothing her arm, nor soothing her with calming words. He would show no approval of this behavior. He began to feel afraid of her. He toweled the sluggish streak of ejaculate off the sheet with a face towel.

He picked up the pink princess phone with one hand, found the missing cord and dialed his mother, Alice, at her workplace. Steve needed her support in getting Sophie help. He felt overwhelmed, and very desperate to guard their privacy, lest his ministry be tainted.

Alice was a person who didn't allow being known by others, especially by Sophie. Steve's dependence on his mother had always been a thorn in Sophie's flesh. Without consulting her, he would call Alice for advice. He would call on Alice to bail them out financially when they met a wall.

Steve's father had done well in oil stocks during the time petroleum was scarce. Shortly after their move from Texas, he was mowing the lawn when he experienced a stroke, severe enough that he didn't ever recover. Alice fed him each evening at the care home and tried to communicate with him as the pureed food drooled down his chin. His quizzical eyes wandered around her face as she fed him. His mouth closed down on the rubber spoon when he was done. Now, Sophie's eyes were like his: angry.

Alice lived very well, but she worked hard. Retirement pay from Mobil and their insurance took good care of them. She continued to work as a CPA. Up at 5:30, and off to the office by 7:00, she expected her employees to put in several hours before the phones began to ring.

Alice stayed in control, always vigilant by nature but more so after Mitchell, her husband, suffered a stroke, which reinforced the many treacheries life had in store.

Steve sat on the edge of their bed beside Sophie as they waited, holding the sheet taut against her struggling arms as they waited for his mother. He gripped them tightly, and they bruised, though Sophie would not notice until later when she was allowed to take her first shower.

She settled. She was quiet; silent tears came into her eyes, but he didn't wipe them away. She knew he didn't understand how she had broken through. She felt forgiveness from God that later would prove to be transient.

How different things could be for them as a couple now that she was a true believer, special to Father God. She understood now the feelings of the worshippers who held their hands in the air. She would sing along, like them as if hypnotized, *"His name is wonderful, Jesus, my Lord."*

Alice came within fifteen minutes. Finding Sophie out of her mind seemed to her like gross irresponsibility on Sophie's part. What were these fantasies she had allowed to develop in her thinking? She had too much time alone, clearly. Why did she insist on going to school again and again, when it was about time they had a child. Books, books, books. She was often cozied up with a book or in the kitchen doing something fanciful.

Alice looked around, saw the smeared blood, and collected the greasy towel, holding it out and away from her as she sought her son and his wife. Going about the house she blew out the candles one by one. She stopped in the doorway to their bedroom and looked in at Sophie and her only son. Steve seemed crumpled and dazed. Something that had lain in her mind as a theory since their courtship, the hunch that they would not be right for each other, was proved the moment she saw them. Sophie was a wreck. Steve held her still on the disheveled and blood stained bed.

Sophie whispered between her short erratic breaths. "Hello Alice."

★★★

Alice went to the car without saying a word to either of them and cleared the front seat of various religious tracts, a MacDonald's wrapper, old coffee, resisting rolling her eyes at Steve's slovenliness.

Sophie shuffled toward the open car door, and her sandals slipped ahead of her. Her soul ached for gentleness even as Steve walked her to the sedan and Alice pushed her head down into it, like a policeman does a criminal during an arrest.

They didn't understand how the truth had finally saturated her soul. The dilapidated levee of doubt had broken! The waters were pummeling her downstream.

Rosella had come out onto her porch in her apron, shielding her eyes, and watching the scene. Sophie felt a sudden and deep love for her kind neighbor and smiled, largely and optimistically. Rosella put her hands to her face.

All those years of angst and unworthiness, and Sophie had never found the solace of inclusion. But now, as the door closed, she felt God's love still with her. Every feeling she'd ever had seemingly found expression in this new unexpected reverie. But they wouldn't understand.

On the way to the nearest Emergency Room she sat between her husband and mother-in-law on the bench of the front seat of the hand-me-down black 1968 Plymouth Alice had given them.

Her sheet caught momentarily in the gear shift and mother and son freed it, both reaching over her, tugging, anxious to be on their way. The nipped toe bled into the sheet and into her sandal. *How could a little toe bleed so much?* She shucked off the sandals they had forced on her feet.

Steve let out the clutch too quickly, and the car lurched forward.

Alice reached in her handbag for a handkerchief and dabbed her hands. She hated the smell of Noxzema. Alice wondered why Sophie smeared a cleansing cream all over her body.

It was rush hour traffic. Evening was closing in. Darkness would come before they arrived at the Emergency Room.

It was just weeks before Christmas. The semester was over and, the business of the holidays had begun for many. The lights in the yards of the neighbors seemed joyful and inspiring.

Sophie hadn't caught the fever to shop and decorate. She had, however, made a four-point average. She had enough credits to matriculate into San Jose College. Finally, she would reach her goal. Even if had to be in spurts. For the moment those academic aspirations had deserted her as the car merged onto the freeway.

She had borrowed tuition money from her parents, explaining to them that she wanted to obtain a degree, if only for herself. They had conceded, and she had felt less under Steve's control.

She liked the autonomy. She met more people and enjoyed her coffee dates with the professor. He had admired her essay on *The Bell Jar*.

Sylvia Plath hadn't found a new life like Sophie had. Sophie would not cower as if enclosed in a jar, not even to God. In this new place, she felt robust and freed from the confining spaces of where she had hidden as a child.

"Sophie, stay still. We're getting you help," Steve said.

Initially, Sophie thrashed between them, immersed in the rush that had overtaken her mind. She shook her head in an exaggerated way, saying, "God touched me. God called me."

Still in Fremont, Steve geared down and pulled just beyond an exit to Mission Boulevard and stopped. Alice was to sit with Sophie in the back seat, allowing Steve to drive safely. Passing cars honked as Alice opened her door cautiously.

In the darkening twilight, Sophie escaped them. She slipped from Alice's grasp and out of her sheet, and ran barefoot and naked between the cars. She crossed the freeway one lane at a time. The drivers braked and swerved, honking and screeching as she crossed. She ran toward home. Instinctively, she ran to some kind of home for her heart.

The highway shoulder was sometimes asphalt and sometimes gravel. She felt the sharp gravel pit her heels. Headlights caught her back and legs in slashes of yellow light, like caution lights flashing on and off. The cars sped by. Rubble and old newspaper pages disturbed by the passing cars floated up and around her. A small rock hit her calf. Still she ran.

Looking back, she saw Alice standing near the car. Steve was verging on crossing the third lane. She ran for home: across the median and through the lanes of honking drivers on the other side. Steve appeared stranded, and she felt strong for having outfoxed him. He was the enemy.

She ran now against the traffic, and the headlights hit her mad face like flashes of lightning. She stayed on the shoulder, and her feet could find no smooth place. *One should always wear shoes,* she thought.

Her breasts bounced as she ran. Her elbows moved in keeping with her pace, no longer a jogger but a runner. She felt hidden, like her vagina, folded beautifully around herself.

Flashing lights were coming toward her. She tried to leave the freeway, but high walls left her no escape.

The California Highway Patrol pulled onto the ramp and circled back; two officers opened their doors simultaneously and burst onto the freeway. She stopped short. Confused, she ran the other way.

The younger of the two officers ran after her, and promptly caught hold of her arm. She fell, her thigh sliding painfully against the asphalt. She gave out a cry. The second officer, holding an emergency blanket caught up with them. They picked her up, each by an arm and wrapped her just as Steve had, in restraining swaddling.

Moving back toward the patrol car, each patrolman held an arm just under the armpit where it hurt. She waddled back between them, the blanket chafing her scraped thigh that felt like a fresh burn.

The young officer pushed her head down as she was tucked into the back seat. Things had gone wrong.

The patrol car sped along the shoulder, past the traffic squeezed together along the highway Sophie had just covered.

Sophie felt despair and a passing awareness of her nudity. She shivered and pulled the rough fabric of the blanket over her legs and shoulders. Then she returned her grip to the cage with both hands, leaning forward.

She shouted through the barrier, "There's my husband. There he is. He's looking for me."

The police pulled over and waited as Steve crossed the highway and approached the vehicle.

"Do you know this woman?" The driving officer asked as he exited the car. "Does she have any identification?"

Steve was standing a short distance from the Plymouth, looking toward the flashing blue lights of the patrol car. They rippled, signaling *beware and avoid: someone is in crisis.*

Steve and he stood together outside the car conversing, their heads close together, speaking loudly above the noise of traffic. Alice came over with the sheet in her arms. It was folded and smooth, belying its stains, as if were fresh from the linen closet.

"Here, officer, she should have something more."

He continued to look at the pad in his hand and didn't look up. As they used the patrolman's flashlight to exchange information, Alice dropped the sheet in front of Steve and returned to the car. Sophie watched her peer nervously about her and slide into the driver's seat. *Oh yes,* she thought. *Alice should do the driving.*

As cars came by on both sides, their headlights caught Sophie's wild, cropped head behind the wire grill. She still gripped it, talking, pleading with the remaining officer who sat in the passenger seat. The blanket was stiff and didn't cover her. The white sheet lay crumpled near Steve's feet.

Traffic had slowed even more than usual. Cars crept past. She hadn't remembered her naked shoulders until one of the freeway drivers rolled down his window and whistled. The officer outside had responded by stuffing the sheet through the back door. Sophie shrugged off the blanket and wrapped herself in it, like it was a shroud. She pulled one corner into a triangle over her head as if she were a saint with a wimple and headdress.

The men outside seemed to have come to some agreement.

"I'll meet you there, then," Steve said. They shook hands.

The patrolman in the passenger seat asked of his partner, "So what in the hell is this about? Is she whacko?"

"If she is, it's the first her husband knew of it. She was acting bizarrely when he found her he says. He's not sure what caused her to go around the bend. She wasn't picking up when he called. This is how he found her, crazed and her mind too muddled to speak coherently. He saw blood and thought perhaps she'd hurt herself."

"Talk about freaky." He crossed his arms and settled back in his seat.

He put his head down to doze, oblivious to their passenger as if it were routine to pluck a naked woman off the freeway. But the first patrolman left his right arm on the seat back and half-turned, checking on Sophie frequently until they reached the Emergency Room in Hayward where the staff was ready with a gurney and blankets. Alice and Steve pulled up shortly after.

★★★

Convinced she had been chosen and would soon be in the arms of the Father, she had been excited, in another realm completely, oblivious to her dangerous physical and mental state. *Why was she being taken away from home? Where was she going now? Surely, to her new home in Heaven.*

One of the officers reached in for her. After a moment she emerged, still sheathed. She kicked the officer in the shins, once, twice, before he restrained her once again. Anger ... she felt a deep visceral clutching anger, and she put on her best scowl. She wanted nothing or no one to interfere with her experience.

The patrolman whom she had kicked spoke soothingly to her in a low, intimate voice. "It's going to be alright. You'll be safe here."

With a sudden melting impulse, she leaned into his shoulder. He held her head against him as her shoulders folded inward. He tipped his head toward hers, as he continued to breathe words near her ear. He led her to the waiting gurney, on which she lay with his help under warmed blankets. He kept a careful eye as he followed. He held her hand until she entered the doors of the brightly lit emergency room. She closed her eyes and never saw his face or thanked him.

The sweetness of having been touched by God returned. She tried to raise herself but found she was held to the bed by wide leather belts.

Those milling about in the ER impatiently waiting their turn to be examined watched as she was wheeled through the waiting room into a small triage treatment room. The waiting patients had turned to talk among themselves as she was being registered. She had whispered as if to herself.

An infant cried, its sounds of distress echoing in the expansive room. The mother stood and shook the baby against her chest and walked toward

Sophie's scene, curious and brazen. Others peered, ignoring the courtesy of giving privacy.

Alice and Steve stood apart, watching, providing the information needed when asked. Alice was the primary on the insurance policy. She signed, and Sophie was admitted to the hospital.

The officer turned and spoke with the uniformed hospital security person who stood at the door, signed some papers and joined his partner in the waiting vehicle. No one but Sophie would remember his gentle way with her.

The admitting doctor at the Emergency Room presented her with a clipboard for her signature. He, too, was gentle with her and looked her in the eyes. She noticed that his eyelids had several folds and they seemed kind. His belly brushed against her coverings. Still panting, she sighed, feeling befriended by him, glad that she had finally become an important part of the process. After a few brief questions, he handed her something to drink that he explained would help her breathe more easily.

"Is this the glory?" she said, convinced now that she was in fact dying and about to receive the commuted garments of the redeemed, the prize of the righteous, reflecting God's glory home at last in the courts of Heaven.

"If that's what you'd like," he nodded, holding the glass to her mouth, tipping it into her throat.

It was cold, freshly squeezed orange juice. She was thirsty and took the glass, drinking the last of it. Between her front teeth she trapped and burst the soft spines of the pulp.

She knew she was dying. It seemed to her in her demented state that death must be necessary to meet the Father and attain Christ-likeness. She would gladly die. Death to self, the minister always instructed: death to all your fleshly desires. Maybe, as he said, by dying she would be 'free of all things carnal' and of the temptations of the flesh the apostle Paul warned against.

Glorified, she would receive the promised new garments in place of her old tattered ones, and they would be whiter than the snow, certainly fresher than the stained sheet in which she had been wrapped. The closed room smelled like Noxzema, still milky on her legs and arms. The thick opalescent cream had seeped into the sheet, making it shiny and wet, causing it to cling to the long straight shape of her hips and narrow torso.

"Thou art with me. . ." she quoted from Psalms 23. Indeed, she was dying.

The gentle doctor on call conferred with the nurse and left, closing the door. She mused: *Was one allowed to be conscious after all, fully aware during the process of dying? No wonder the Psalmist described death as the Valley of the shadow.* She straightened her back, proud to be so brave. They dressed her in a blue cotton gown. She stretched out her hands as they put it on. Alice helped by covering her and tying it in a firm knot in the back.

Warm blankets were put beneath those placed before. Here was the sweetness of preparation. She would be presented to the Father ... the Bride of Christ. Joy flushed through her and filled the void, transforming her thoughts into a tranquil, softly swirling pond. Gone was the momentum of the gushing, angry river around her.

Her breathing slowed. Her heart beat less strongly. Andre Segovia might have strummed the sweet rhythm she heard. The person dressed in white at her side might not be an angel, but he was kind and welcoming. She smiled.

The blue gown was temporary she knew, but it felt light and comfortable. She was no longer naked or bound in the sheet. Indeed, she began breathing with an appreciation for each breath she inhaled. Her mind fixed on the rise and fall of her chest. Slowly, she descended into a hazy bliss. She exhaled. Her head fell to one side.

While Sophie slept an RN stopped the dwindling bleeding and cleaned and dressed her dirty feet and wounded toe. Alice disposed of the sheet in a red bag that said HAZARDOUUS WASTE and collected her clutch bag. She had avoided Sophie's attempt at eye contact and had said almost nothing during the entire ordeal. Steve had likewise been reticent to engage with his wife or his mother. Sophie was asleep now and they needn't try. He believed he was responsible and hadn't kept a careful eye.

"I had to park in the garage," Steve said, his voice rough, as they left together. His mother led the way as he reached into his pocket to give her the parking ticket. She already had the keys.

★★★

The Bayside Sanitarium where Sophie was transported after the examination was a long distance from Saint Mary's Hospital where she would be admitted, especially in heavy traffic. She awoke briefly, to find herself being jostled into a cold, empty van. She couldn't know how long she had slept; there was no daylight by then.

She heard the metal scrape against metal as the gurney slid into place, like the noise of a coffin being locked in a hearse. This was the Valley of the Shadow. But a valley was not a vacuum, and she would come through.

She hadn't known one could be witness to one's own burial. As she was transported in the cold, non-emergency van, she hummed, hazily, "*Just as I am and waiting not … I come.*"

She wanted to believe she was being escorted, although she was alone. She had no familiar thing with her. She felt weakly for the pearl necklace. Her arm was flaccid. She didn't reach her neck, where it was not.

There were no lights except a strobe that swept over her again and again then went away. She was reminded of the car salesmen who advertised with big lights that swiped the sky when she was a child and they went to Portland to see their grandmother who baked pies behind a window at Yaw's Topnotch, for all to see that the pies the restaurant sold were indeed home-made. Sophie enjoyed the smoothness of her thoughts, coming one atop the other. If the dam in her heart had broken, she knew now she had gone smoothly with its flow, its pent-up power just like her own, released and free-flowing now.

Is paradise also a sphere like the earth where one plants one's feet and gravity holds them fast to the ground? Will it have a molten center or is paradise more like empty space, so vague that nothing holds feet to the earth, but rather one is like a spirit, soundless, breathless, and only sensitive to other spirits, indulging and kind?

39

But kindness in such a place would have no contradiction, like condescension or evil with which to compare it. All of the virtues would be of the same tenor, alike in voice, alike in gesture because one would have no contrasting memory of evil and badness. How unscarred would be the memory and how much space for pure goodness, capacity only for good. It would be a new beginning without the hazards. But what is good? Is goodness always tainted by ulterior motives?

For that matter one's whole vocabulary would change unless one had memories of life on earth. The word peace, for instance, wouldn't need to be expressed if there were no contrasting feelings. What a bizarre idea to do away with reactions like fear or the restlessness of residing with anxiety. So few antonyms, such simplicity. No guessing, no wondering or searching for a life purpose. Where would be the marvel of nature, the overwhelming joy of discovery, where would be the challenges to live each day to its fullest?

Briefly, Sophie wanted not to die but to live with the resilience she felt was alive in her. She couldn't imagine the consequences of death, except that nothing would be required of her except to be. Or maybe, eternal worship of the Father was what was expected?

There will be no steeples reaching up toward God, no cathedrals built on the backs of serfs, no spires, no sacrificial fires with smoke ascending toward Heaven, no grottos with enshrined saints. No stations of the cross, no Savior, no Comforter.

She was thinking clearly now, she believed, and was suddenly sick not to live her life out, not to solve everyday problems and be more than a sub-being to a God she couldn't imagine and a husband she couldn't know. She stretched back and arched her back, in anguish, remorseful now to leave her life.

People would be able to see her dead body. No one could know that she was alive and courageous about going through the Valley of the Shadow of Death. She sank away again in fearful anticipation of what was next.

The gurney was hard and rattling as the van rumbled on. She felt the pull in her body as the driver braked. When he accelerated she felt the drag. Then she neither felt nor heard anything as she fell back into darkness and dreamed we cannot know what.

★★★

Her husband and his mother had followed the van in the car. They signed papers, but didn't follow the gurney inside the locked doors. Later they made a call into the hospital but took the advice of the admitting doctor. They did not come to see her.

The nurses could not wake her, finally resorting to the Glasgow Coma Scale which confirmed she was in a coma. When the doctor came, he inflicted pain on the bottom of her foot with a tongue depressor. There was no reaction. They called her name, but she didn't hear. They opened her eyes, shone a flashlight at them, and the pupils shrank. They shot from side to side. Her brain was active. Sometimes she lay shaking or jerking spasmodically.

A summary of her status came about:

Dehydrated

Low blood pressure

Anemia

High glucose

Low potassium.

Most patients who were admitted to the sanitarium were still paranoid or violent. Some came timidly like little children responding shyly to grownups. She came wholly unconscious.

A bolus of Haldol was administered through the intravenous line, lest she waken and be psychotic and out of control. She was put on two liters of oxygen, the transparent cannula taped into place across the bridge of her nose. The tubing was coiled and attached to the bed rail. The IV would boost her blood pressure. They left her bed in the hall near the nurses' station in order to observe her with a careful eye. Where was she during that unconscious time? Where did her active mind take her? Did she see the bared

41

teeth of a fox or the flared nostrils of a bull, or were there sweet zephyrs and clover in the fields, roses in a hedge? Did doves nest about or was the earth comprised of ashes and the dust of ashes? Were there withered tendrils unable to recuperate from drought? Was Wagner's music subsidiary to the drama that unfolded? Perhaps what she heard was jangled and incoherent, not music at all. Or maybe taunting whispers or mocking haunted her.

★★★

From the shadow of her valley, she woke three days later. An IV pole in tow, she was being supported down a long, narrow, glass hallway, partially shadowed by Japanese Maples in a manicured courtyard split by narrow meandering walkways like those in an abbe.

When she forced her drugged eyelids open, she saw that further ahead, sunlight broke the shadow and cut diagonally across the oak handrail she was gripping. As a girl when she was swinging she loved going up from the shadow of the cedar into the brighter sunshine where she saw the sky below. She was intent on reaching the sunlight and feeling its warmth on her skin.

She shoved her sluggish hand ahead as she went, leaning, stretching forward and grasping toward the light. The man walking her out of her stupor was large and black. He held her around her shoulders and helped her as she determined to reach the diamond-shaped sunlight that was now just a few steps away. She let go his arm and held the rail with both hands. She stopped, feeling she had achieved something when she grasped the sunlit rail, but he moved her along as if she had yet to accomplish something.

He continued walking her out of the Haldol-induced stupor, not knowing where she would be psychologically when she truly came around.

It may have been that she was slight or the Doctor had misjudged the dose administered in the orange juice at the ER, whatever it was. Mistakes had been made in the transfer of patient information from the ER to the Bayside Sanitarium. For three days she had lain in a bed in the hallway, well in sight, deaf to the worried murmuring of the nurses. She had slipped beneath consciousness and remained there for those three days, like Lazarus in His tomb.

Now she was assigned to Abe, a nurse practitioner, who walked her and would manage her care.

But she had no other map to go by but the one she had assumed the day she was admitted.

"I'm here then," she said, assuming that where she had come was where the dead should be.

"You're here and safe," Abe, said

"When will I see the Father?"

Abe was strong. She needed his strength. She gripped his bicep. "Thank you," she said.

He seemed consoling, though she didn't believe she needed consolation. She did need a guide in this new place, however. She thought of Dougie, her oldest brother, riding her on his shoulders through the trails in the woods, where otherwise she might have become lost.

"Your father will soon be here," Abe said.

Sophie's heart lurched, and she stammered, "B ... but I meant God, the Father."

Abe knew that Sophie would best make her transition back to reality in a measured way. She would heal far better if she could put things back together piece by piece for herself.

"We'll talk over the next few days," he answered, "and I think I'll be able to answer your questions better."

To Abe, her bearing spoke of sophistication, not of someone who had entered in and out of bouts of psychosis. He did not assume she was schizophrenic or manic-depressive. This seemed to be an acute incident, a separation from reality triggered by what, he did not yet know. His challenge was to find the real person, search out her inner needs and bring her back to sanity, even if the truth that was buried at the root of it proved painful to her.

He had bathed her while she slept. He scrubbed the dark left-over stain of asphalt from her feet and removed the tiny pieces of embedded glass. He saw the fingerprints of bruises on her arm. The long burn on her thigh from sliding on the highway still bled slightly as he washed over it. There was no evidence she had been raped. He didn't know the history of these foreboding markings.

It was not enough to hear her story from others. Only she could tell it. He needed to start with her sense of reality. Time was required, and he knew not to rush her.

Sophie didn't find herself exactly where she had expected, but she reasoned that much depended on facing the hard part of being dead, the mystery of it all. It was a strange place. The walls were bare. Beds and wheel chairs, lined up against them waiting.

She had nothing of her own. Her opal ring was gone. She toyed with the indentation on her finger where she usually found the soft, azure stone of her grandmother's ring. It once brought comfort and the fond memories of feeling special to someone.

The pearl was missing too, but she continued to feel for it and often left her hand at her neck.

Who was Abe, on whom she relied entirely? He seemed ready to explain, but she didn't know the questions to ask.

These delays in what was to come, what she believed would be the celebration of her home—coming, were the hardest part so far. Perhaps there was a stop-off before one was welcomed through the gates. Perhaps this was Purgatory where the last purification would be accomplished. Surely being conscious meant she had risen. But no one seemed to realize she should see the Father

She wondered aloud to him, "Am I in the right place?"

Abe flinched at the question. It seemed too soon to tell her that she was institutionalized.

"Where do you think you are?" He asked.

She asked again to be presented to the Father.

"I'm home now, shouldn't I see Him?"

Abe turned to uncoil the IV tubing and busied himself until the question was no longer on her lips or in her expression.

If she could see the Father, she would also see His Son on the right hand. That should be the natural course of events, she thought, after one dies. She was certain that the trickle of fear that was beginning to drop, drop, drop into the fibers of her heart after waking would dissolve into pure air once she was standing in the light of the Trinity's holiness and grace.

She felt her fear cringing and slinking away just as something evil would in the magnificence of His perfect presence. Joy would displace every other feeling, especially those little ones that remained of the natural world. Anna and she would be reunited, because Anna was going to die too, and it was okay now. There was really no other way it could be.

Sophie determined to make something happen. So far her only encounter with anyone, human or divine had been with Abe. She picked her tender feet up from the bed and shuffled up to the prescription window. Abe, in white jacket and pants, stood back, his arms crossed.

An older man with a full head of gray hair, also dressed in all white, stood beside a counter in the distance. He glanced toward her as she leaned in. He could see that she stood on the tips of her toes.

He was not at all how she expected God to look, but she pursued the idea the man was He.

The glass window slid open, and she asked a man dressed in all blue to see the Father. She wondered momentarily if she were acting appropriately, but willingly abandoned her doubt in the interests of her new faith. It was all about faith. Being here was proof. Small communion cups were lined up next to the young man in blue scrubs. He checked his clipboard and looked at her arm band.

"May I see the Father?"

"Your father's not here and, it's not time for your medications," he said, dropping her arm and sliding the glass window shut.

She knocked. The man in the back turned from the counter where he worked and said, "Come back in two hours, and it will be time for your medications."

After she let go his gaze, he looked at her longer as if he knew her. The window slid open again so she could make out what he was saying. He spoke from a distance.

Perhaps she was mistaken. It should have come about simply and easily, seeing the Father. Thinking that it might not be her turn, she asked through the window, "Are there others waiting?"

"Waiting? Waiting for what?" His voice was louder now.

Her mind found a cubby hole, like a nest built for pigeons, unyielding and artificial: tin boxes discolored by white droppings and punctuated by lost feathers and protruding bits of straw.

Abe, the one who had helped walk her in the shadowed hallway into the bright light, had known this moment would come. He had seen it before. He knew she would soon begin to experience tiny shocks of reality, and he intended to be there when the full current snapped through her and she understood where she was.

Abe knew the dangers of believing too strongly, becoming fanatical, and wanting to express or test your faith. When one committed to it wholeheartedly, it inevitably caused an upheaval of the mind now out of touch with reality, rendered incapable of reason, unable to distinguish the imaginary from the real, stressed past coping.

He wondered about her hair. The copper tones in the sprouts that were left shimmered under the bright lights near the medicine counter.

Her pale face was reflected on the glass from the darker interior where the pharmacist still studied her.

She looked at herself: her wide eyes, her chopped hair, and touched the glass where the lines in her face pulled down. She didn't have her natural coloring. She turned to Abe, her hand atop her head.

"What did I do to myself?" She ran her hand down the scraped skin of her scalp.

★★★

Abe wanted to prepare Sophie as best he could for the pain of discovering she had been admitted into a locked down institution, an asylum.

It was not at all uncommon for patients to have a fixation on God; they were sure they had received a message; either that or they knew they had been invited by an alien to leave this earth on a space ship parked on their lawn under the moonlight. He didn't begin by debunking a patient of his or her ideas.

There were those patients who could repeat verbatim the strange prompting voices they had heard at times in other languages. Sometimes they obeyed the voices. Some believed evil spirits had possessed them, their demons' presence sometimes almost as real to Abe. But given his twenty-five years and more of practice, he was inured to the preposterous ideas. Either there would be a better outcome or there wouldn't. Only with the passing of time, could they tell.

There were patterns and a degree of predictability in the behavior and mania of his patients. He came to know them and puzzled and designed the sometimes serpentine road home to sanity as best he knew how ... with acceptance and patience. He had an intelligent, careful eye.

Perhaps she would tell him her story. When he listened, he sometimes saw a way to help his patients not only escape their delusions, but also salvage their self-esteem, so that a new appreciation came into their possession. Having been nearly crushed, comparable to yellowing bruises, the mind was restoring itself: many began to recuperate.

Other patients would become permanent residents of that mysterious place the mind can go, where untimely synapses and chemical imbalances can destroy a personality, where no one knows you anymore and you can't abide the present or make provision for your future. Unlucky ones sit on the street in cities like Paris, London or New York stretched out across the pavement, an empty cup extended in one hand. One hopes, if not for healing, then at least for a place of protection of such souls.

He preferred that his patients have no visitors before they understood they were in an institution. Except for those who were schizophrenic or even psychopathic, he believed most of his patients would come through their turmoil once they had been given care and time.

The inherent humiliation of being brought here in such a disoriented state was hard to overcome. Sophie seemed to him especially fragile. She was trying hard to keep her illusions and a sense of dignity in place. If the illusions were severed in a coup de grace, she might lose her sense of being in control of her mind.

Some visitors triggered feelings the patient didn't need to own: guilt, shame, or responsibility for the actions of others. Some relationships were just plain toxic, and the cause of their breakdown. One day the effect of these relationships would be neutralized if the patient was able to walk away tall again, hopeful.

But, poison can seem like nectar. His patients had to begin to distinguish again among their family and friends who best respected and bolstered them. Abe knew: *The slow slaughter of the egos of children takes place every day in homes near and far in every culture. Coping later, those children become adults to face an uneven playing field. Sometimes painful separations were necessary for the patient to survive and move forward.*

Abe was patient with the process, recognizing turning points, catching the moment a patient's eyes looked to him to silently confirm that a fraction of understanding had come.

The pastor came unexpectedly the day after she woke up. *"Why was he here when she was no longer among the living?"* Sophie wondered. Her conclusions were losing credence every moment.

It had been the psychiatrist's idea to allow the requested visit; he had been open to the idea of a panacea. Abe had disagreed, insisting that he and Sophie needed to talk before she met with the pastor. The pastor was willing to wait. Abe took his time. The pastor waited for over an hour.

★★★

On a garden bench, Abe leaned over, looking up at Sophie. A shaft of light caught the bare spaces in her scalp.

Even though prematurely in his way of thinking he began very simply, "Sophie, everything seems strange to you because you broke apart emotionally. You didn't die as you believe. This is a hospital. You were brought to this institution to receive care until you're strong enough emotionally to leave, until you're rational again."

Sophie couldn't hear the words. Her own truth still ruled her.

Abe knew that more time was needed. Dr. Savoire had been mistaken. It was too early to break apart her invented world. The question of why she had invented it was still unanswered.

"Over time when you exhibit normal behavior, you'll be released. You may stay in treatment as an outpatient, but you'll go home again. I believe we can shoot for a day home for Christmas. I need you to begin telling me your story."

★★★

Sophie began, haltingly at first, to tell Abe how it came about that she had died.

"But you're not dead, Sophie. You have your life to live."

"Anna is dying."

"But you're not. You're living, though your life will never be the same again after this experience. It will change you. If we work together, you can, in the future, direct your own course and become who you feel you are."

Still, she didn't let go the idea that she was in another place, approximate to Heaven, but not yet Heaven.

She told Abe about the gift her brothers had given her, the tiny pearl necklace. She sobbed and could go no further. "I promised them I wouldn't tell on them about the raft."

"Tell whom, Sophie, who?"

She just shook her head quietly.

"Okay, we'll go slowly and pick up where we left tomorrow or the next, whenever you're ready. But for right now, you must go into the main lobby and meet with Pastor Billings, just past the locked doors."

"Why am I locked in when this is supposed to be my resting place? And you're saying I didn't die? Then where am I, and why am I here?"

"You've had a breakdown, Sophie, an emotional breakdown. We don't know why."

Sophie felt she wasn't ready to meet the minister, but Abe showed her to a metal double door that opened into a grand lobby. She stood agape. Being led to meet him, seeing the fire proof doors, seeing the grandness of the room, was the first moment that she realized she had been behind locked doors all this time. She looked to Abe. Abe nodded, answering the question in her eyes.

He stepped back into the restricted area after turning her over to an orderly. Just outside the double locked doors, the minister pulled his jacket down and straightened his blue paisley tie. The tie was narrow as was fashionable. The three of them, Sophie, the pastor and the orderly, walked together toward some seating in front of a large fireplace with logs, behind which had been arranged a spray of pine boughs and holly. The orderly stopped and stood a short distance away. She and the pastor sat in large arm chairs opposite each other. She kept her hands clasped in her lap.

Sophie's feet had slipped out of the green slippers as she walked. When she sat, she held her feet to the floor so her bruised soles wouldn't be noticeable. She remembered the freedom she had experienced as she ran from the car that evening, and wished she could run now. She brushed her hand against the scab on her arm, hardened and ready to come off. She had disturbed it several times. There was a ring of red around it. She suddenly felt ashamed that she habitually picked her scabs. She had no sleeve to hide it.

Even the smell was different from the corridor from where she'd come. She lifted the front of her gown and smelled deeply. She didn't know how Heaven would smell, but certainly it smelled differently than her gown.

Perhaps the pastor had been sent to introduce her to the Father. It was all another world to her. The puzzle was tedious, the pieces too tiny; the colors bled together into undifferentiated tones, the shapes all alike. It was beyond her. She had presumed she had died, but, now it seemed doubtful. Perhaps this was the precipice to Hell? *Hell might have its immediate pleasures,* she considered. *Even briefly so you could confabulate what the deprivations would be thereafter.* She thought of Rodin's Gates of Hell. Inspired by Dante, Rodin's sculptures of them depicted something different entirely. *No this did not seem like Hell.*

If she believed in one though, did she believe in the other? *Heaven and hell, strapped in the sky, waiting for occupants? Surely, she would be judged guilty. She was the cause of so much tragedy. Despite her cravings for forgiveness and her confessions, she couldn't be forgiven. She shouldn't.*

The pictures hanging on the walls were of noble looking riders in boots and tailored habits astride noble looking horses. The grass in the pictures was extremely green and stretched over infinite hills to the horizon. Another had huge magnolias. There were Currier and Ives reproductions: pastel pictures of lone ships, their sails broad to the wind.

Chandeliers hung about, and one giant cluster of crystals dangled above a large vase filled with sprawling blue hydrangeas. None of this seemed heavenly. It was gaudy.

The faux Duncan Phyfe table was round and had legs capped with metal, open-mouthed beasts that reminded her of things evil and lurking. She was uncomfortable, yet she still felt the pulling thread of hope, even though fear had tangled with it. It was a wrenching, tenuous hope.

She recalled the night she came to be here: the dark van ride inside its cavernous metal belly. As if by a leviathan, she thought, she'd been swallowed whole. How Jonah must have trembled when he realized he was in the dark belly of a whale. Turning toward the east, he prayed until he was spewed onto the shore. *What direction should she turn? Who could understand where she'd been and what she had experienced? Surely, not Pastor Billings, sitting rigidly in his suit and tie. Like Steve, throughout the ordeal, she remembered, he did not meet her eyes.*

"Shall we pray?" he said.

"No need, I'm about to meet the Father. I just have to wait. I'm surprised you're here. I have passed. Why are you here?" She tried out her truth on him, testing it, not as sure as before but persisting in it.

The pastor sat back then leaned forward and took her arm.

"I rebuke you Satan, in the name of the Father, the Son and the Holy Ghost. Drive out this demon and bring her out of her torment."

"That's all been taken care of. I was told we're safe here." She scowled.

"It will take spiritual warfare to restore your mind, Sophie. You've been possessed. There are demons posing as angels in control of your spirit and mind. Only through the Holy Spirit can you be delivered. You have to be willing to have them exorcised. We used the prayer chain. Many in the congregation have gathered together in the sanctuary today while I'm here to pray for your deliverance. No doctor here can heal you. Only God delivers from evil."

"My mind and heart are right with God," she said.

She was uneasy that people were gathered at the church to pray for her. Surely it was a wake. Head down, she listened on, twisting in her seat, wringing her hands.

"Sophie, you've been irresponsible and haven't taken charge of your own spiritual welfare. The scripture says to take on the full armor of God. Satan has taken advantage of you. You weren't on guard."

His voice echoed around the quiet room and reached several elderly people in similar gowns to Sophie's who were slumped along a wall. They raised their heavy heads, gazing at Sophie and her pastor. Then they shrank back and seemed to be waiting as if for a train or a bus. One man sat erect and held both hands atop his cane. He cocked his head quickly to listen, like a rooster might.

"We all must live out our lives responsibly. We must constantly battle the spirits of evil. You've got to become responsible for your own spiritual journey. Satan is good at what he does to destroy a soul."

The demented old man, his out of place cap to one side, thumped his cane several times. He was looking at them intently now, agitated. He may have believed she was possessed.

She broke off the dialogue. How could anyone be so insensitive to the spiritual world she had discovered? Responsible? She had done all she knew to take responsibility. No one could have been more earnest than she.

She began to see in the corner of her mind, that she had been left to journey here alone. No one had soothed her; no one had told her where she was going; no one seemed to even acknowledge who she was. Would she be vomited by the whale, like Jonah, onto the shore still alone and distraught, but wanting to be obedient? Why was she trapped?

Or was she being transmuted to something precious, from human to heavenly? Would a chariot come for her as it had for the prophet Elijah? She had believed the transformation would be in the twinkling of an eye. Perhaps there is a process.

Only Abe had met her eyes the whole time. His dark eyes set amongst permanent wrinkles, were the only tenderness she'd found here. There were no callouses on his soul. He didn't attribute her condition to evil spirits or irresponsibility. She wanted to be safe, back behind those doors. What was true? What could Abe show her?

Facts and fiction began to polarize. She could feel the collision of what she thought and what in fact the truth was as she began to understand it. She realized she was truly locked-in, not in splendid courtyards, but in a sterile place that smelled like scorched milk. Even a geranium smelled better. She began crying. The jostling of opposing ideas had left her stranded in no place.

She wondered what condition it was that she was in that brought a pastor of a large congregation to see her when he hadn't taken her calls the day she had pleaded with the secretary to see him. She had pled to no avail.

She allowed such bits of logic to reconstruct her situation. How could she be dead and talking with the pastor at the same time? She was so very sure she had died.

Her reality was no longer verifiable. The wires were crossed. The lines were jammed. She crossed her arms on the green velvet chair, burying her face in them. She couldn't remember wandering so far in the wilderness of her mind.

The pastor nodded to the orderly, and walked just behind her to the locked double doors. He left her while tears still dropped from her eyes. With the push of a button, she was no longer on soft green carpet but back in the long tiled hallway. Abe stood waiting for her and gently took her elbow.

As they walked by, the glass window slid soundlessly open. The pharmacist handed her one of the little paper cups the size used for communion wine and said, "Take them here where I can observe you."

She did. "Is there no wine with the broken bread?" She took the large chalky pills certainly not administered commemorating His shed blood. She let the water linger in her throat. She was weak, and her hand shook when she handed back the paper cup.

She examined her gown. The hem was loose on the right sleeve. How could she have even begun to think this was a holy place? Ashamed and embarrassed, she covered her face with her hands. How could she have imagined he was God? He was not the Father. He was a pharmacist. He would not forgive her. This was not the splendid courtyard she had imagined.

★★★

Shame, even undeserved shame, has no easy exit from the mind. It abides and tarnishes what is most pure. Exposure to shame damages and erodes the spirit irrefutably just as beautiful silver objects will oxidize as they are exposed to the world. Our remorse, the overwhelming nature of shame, is like struggling in water with cumbrous mud filled boots.

Shame comes as an impostor dressed in the garb of the need for repentance. It cannot be shrugged off, except by the consistent kindness, the consolation of forgiveness, the acknowledgement and acceptance of someone else that sees the "you" you are, who sees the face you can only touch but never see directly. By grace are we saved.

We may limp, but we walk the earth the best we know. Often we are a contradiction to ourselves. Abe saw her trying to shuck the damning boots that would drown her.

Abe saw that she hung her head and covered her face, that shame and remorse coursed sluggishly through her mind like gross silt in a dark pond, with too little current to bring it life. Long held shame doesn't wash away easily.

Shame is often infectious, easily transmitted in childhood when the way others see you and protect ... or fail to protect you . . . provide your only environment.

The soul is needy, and Abe saw she was in need of acceptance, a spiritual essence that can only come from another human.

She is losing Anna. Who else but he could follow her crooked path back? Single file. She had to go single file, but he would divine the road from behind as best he could, and prompt her when she got off-course. This was a starting point.

Abe knew that shame and guilt were addictive, that they provided a sure place of retreat from real life for the mind. Abstention, learning not to retreat under shame's cover and not to make guilt one's sole diet, would be required until the habit to live openly and feast from the buffet of life's pleasures could be acquired.

Abe also knew that an awareness of where one's thoughts go, whether unconsciously or by default was key to forming new habits. After recognizing the pattern, Sophie could consciously direct her thinking differently and reject that shelter in her mind where the stench of shame prevails.

First, Abe would need to know when the habit began. Was there an event? When did she enter that dimly lit cave of self-loathing?

His big feet were planted beside her as she looked down. The heavy shoes were white and the white laces were double knotted. Her own were green and disposable. She wanted shoes for outdoors, not paper slippers. Again, she wanted to run, as if by instinct she would know her destination, but she knew this time that she wasn't equipped to run and that the doors were locked.

"The pastor said, I'm possessed by the Devil, Abe. He said I need to be delivered. All of these people have gathered at the church to pray for my deliverance. I'm embarrassed to think they're all talking about what happened to me. I can never go back there to that church. I'm mortified. What will the pastor confide to Steve? I wonder if Alice will advise him to leave me."

"We'll get it sorted out, but let's go to the music room now and you can let the music fill your thoughts for a while."

Sophie shuffled beside Abe, under his kind, large hand.

★★★

Later, they were alone in the music room ready to put their head phones on. Looking at her directly Abe said, "May I tell you how you came to be here?"

Sophie looked at Abe. "Yes, I want to know how."

"You were taken to the emergency room in Hayward. Your husband had come home and found you delirious and unintelligible. He and his mother bound you in a sheet and brought you to the nearest hospital Emergency Room.

"You were medicated and brought here to us, medicated pretty heavily, I might add. This is a facility for people who lose their way, most often temporarily. It can be a respite.

"You were unconscious for three days. According to your chart, when you were taken to Hayward ER you were incoherent and possibly a danger to yourself," Abe said. "You gave your consent to be hospitalized before you were medicated. They may not have advised you in a way that you understood at the time. Beyond that, you were physically exhausted."

He saw the cheeks, wet now with tears weaving down her face. She swiped at them. He was her mirror, and there was a quiet timbre in his voice, a tender understanding in his face which gave way to a thin reassuring smile. It was not sympathy. She felt safe with him. She asked nothing further. It was enough to know she had been judged insane and locked up. A tenuous smile flitted about her mouth as she placed the headphones over her ears.

Closing her eyes to listen to a recording of Clair de Lune, she tried to fill in some of the blank spaces in her memory. But for the moment, she couldn't tolerate memories, she could only be soothed by the music. As the music played, she felt ready to nurse herself back to health, to respect her physical body for what it could and could not do. She was alive, after all, and the challenge was hers.

Hope seeped into her spirit from Abe's confidence and concern. He was listening to the same music, in his own mind in awe of its beauty, but present too with Sophie. She wondered what she could learn from this large man, and what made him so prescient. She would try to go to those memories, and she would rummage through the ones she had barricaded from when she was a child years ago. *It will hurt,* she thought. It felt as if the piano strings were strung in her heart.

"We've assigned you a longer-term room. You'll have a roommate later today."

His hand went lightly around her shoulder as they walked in the small garden, but the path became narrow and she had to lead. He followed, catching her question. "How can I begin to heal when I'm so hazy from the medications?

A tic had developed around her right eye. She swiped at the jumping nerve.

"We'll sort out your story in the days to come. I'd like to hear more of your background. It's important."

Still talking, she stood with Abe at the entry to her door and looked back at the garden. No wonder there was a garden In the Beginning.

The patients had unusual habits. One carried a blanketed baby doll on her shoulder. She bedded it on the hard plastic seat next to her, leaned over and talked to it, rearranging the blanket to cover its hands which stuck straight out.

Sophie had a doll she loved, she remembered that clearly: she was dark skinned and made of rubber. Why did Amosandra, one of her few belongings, come to mind as she watched this grown woman pretend she had a baby? She wondered about loving Amosandra, while all the while it was the butt of her mother and brothers' jokes, and maybe others as well.

She secretly adopted a kitten in her childhood and other strays. Once a bird had fallen, and she tried to keep it while it healed but when she pulled the Band Aid away from its feathers she could see how contorted it was. The broken wing didn't heal and later she had found it on it back, legs straight in the air. The life had gone out of it, and it was hideous. Still she touched the bird as if to waken it. Maybe she loved Amosandra because no one else did.

"Sophie has a nigger baby. Sophie has a nigger baby," her brothers had chanted all the time.

As she observed the other patients, she found herself captivated by Lily, a thin woman in street clothes carrying a black out-of-style leather handbag on her arm. Sophie could hear the sharp snap of the clasp open and shut. She continuously walked back and forth at a fast clip. Her heels tapped on the hard tile. There was no rhythm to the combined sounds. Still opening and closing her purse, she stopped by Sophie to tell her that her son would be here soon.

"He's grown and now he takes care of me. I'm ready for him to come take me to the city. I've been ready all day."

She hurried away. Click, click, clickclickclick.

A bent-over male patient, greasy black hair across his forehead, had paced with an unlit cigarette in his mouth. He walked the hallway to the locked doors back and forth. The cigarette was limp and off-colored. He moved it around his lips as he said, "Time to go. Time to go." Over and over he said the same thing. Sometimes he stopped, removed the cigarette and said it more emphatically, "Time to go; Time to go."

The radio frequency came through another patient's hearing aids, crackling and whistling loudly enough to be heard by passersby, but he was apparently used to the screeching. He held his hand to one ear, and the tiny microphone shrieked back.

A stolid young woman, seated on a bench by the window, her blonde hair tied in a knot, was bent at the waist with her hands on her head. When she pounded one side with her fist, the nearby RN took her arm and helped her stand.

Let's go back to your room for a bit," Joanie, her nurse said. "Are you thirsty? There's ice water in your room."

Sophie began her story with how she came to be friends with Anna.

★★★

1950

The first graders squirmed to be outdoors, but the lesson had just begun. An intensely sunny day followed by others came rarely. Indian summer, they called it, when a rainy August was followed by a sun-filled September.

"*No fair, no fair,*" they said.

Sophie sat behind Anna on that first day of school. She was a spectacle because of the tragedy. When she came in the room grew suddenly quiet. Light streamed in and caught the classroom full of innocent faces in complete sunshine. She blinked. She saw no seats left. It was almost time for the bell at eight.

Anna looked back, noticing Sophie adjusting to the sight before her. Behind Anna was an empty desk. The top that lifted was not properly aligned and slanted sideways. No one else had taken it. Anna motioned. Sophie walked in and kept her eyes on Anna, needing a desk so badly in this frightening moment.

Anna sensed she also needed a friend. Anna knew everyone because they had all been to kindergarten together. It was in those moments when Sophie realized she hadn't been told about kindergarten. She felt tricked by her mother, but strangely enough, not by her father. The tragedy that had just transpired in her life draped over her like a heavy blanket. She kept her head down, except to thank Anna.

Sophie and Anna were seated in the second row near the front. She noticed Anna's green wool jumper, the shade of a green pasture. The sweater under it was also green, but its knitted texture made its tone seem lighter.

Anna's thick braids were long. The variety of blond tones all woven together reminded Sophie of her dream horse, a Palomino, which would have a white mane and tail.

Anna often swung them to the back, maybe to get them out of her way, first one and then the other. Tiny green barrettes were clipped over the rubber bands on the end of each pigtail. Sometime, Anna would put one barrette in her mouth and move it around, especially when she had one elbow on her desk. She sucked on the very end of it. Sophie wanted to feel the plastic in her own mouth.

Mrs. Wendt drew three straight lines on the black board, using a yardstick, and a fresh piece of chalk. She wrote a capital 'A' that reached to the top line. She wrote the small 'a' between the lower lines. They were told to practice, but Sophie had no supplies, not even a pencil.

Anna had everything. She lifted her desk and pulled out a fat pad of paper with a Red Indian Chief on the cover. She sharpened her pencil with her own sharpener. She didn't have to walk to the wall and use the pencil sharpener in front of everyone.

Sophie noticed other things while Anna's desk was propped open: a ruler, a new box of eight crayons, a pink eraser, drawing paper, even a compass to make circles. She had a special bag for her pencils. The tips of the erasers were all clean with no smudges. Sophie smelled the banana that couldn't fit in her decorated lunch pail: Trigger, Dale Evans and Roy Rogers with lariats swinging in a circle in the air riding at a gallop.

There were lines in Anna's pad. She didn't have to draw her own as Sophie had done at home on butcher paper. Anna began to copy what was on the board. Turning, she saw that Sophie hadn't started. The teacher was already putting up a 'B'.

"We're supposed to start copying what's on the board," she said.

"I don't have any paper or pencil, either one," Sophie said.

"How come?"

"I didn't know we were supposed to bring it."

"Use some of mine," Anna said.

Carefully she pushed back the binding of her pad of paper so the pages wouldn't tear at the top when she pulled them loose. She sharpened a pencil, dark green like the color of her barrettes, then turned and put the pencil and smoothed-out paper in front of Sophie.

"Thank you," Sophie whispered.

"No talking, please," Mrs. Wendt said with her back turned to the class.

There were twenty-seven first-graders in the room. Sophie felt they all turned to look at her.

Now the girls were behind and had to catch up, but they both knew their *ABC*'s. They caught up quickly, reaching *Q* before recess. Sophie also used cursive. The *Q*'s were so different. She wondered why. She put a cursive *Q* on her tablet in the margin. Maybe Mrs. Wendt would know she knew all of this already.

Sophie and Anna didn't get to the swings fast enough to be first, but when it was their turn, Sophie pushed Anna as high as she could. Anna didn't know how to push very well. She didn't have brothers who taught you these things. Sophie told her to just pull down on her legs when she swung back instead of just pushing the seat. That way they got higher than the others. The swing would stutter at the highest point. The sky below was blue. The little jolt was part of the thrill.

Anna said, "I know you're sad. Everybody knows you're sad. Will you have your stuff tomorrow?"

Sophie's tears were whisked away as they walked toward a sloping field of grass after taking turns on the swings.

"You won't be sad for always."

But Sophie knew she would.

"It depends on whether my mother needs to go to town. We have to wait until Daddy gets home with the car. If it's not a special trip and not just a waste of gas, then I think she'll go. Sometimes she goes to the locker for meat."

Anna said, "I've got extra." She swung her braids back. Sophie wished she could grow braids. Instead her curls sprang up all over the place as though there had been no attempt to style them.

"Much easier to wash that way," her mother had said, when she cut it again. "It grows like a weed. This way I don't have to comb out the tangles."

Sometimes Sophie tried combing it out with water to make it straight.

Her mother would say, "What have you done to your hair?"

"How long is your hair?" Sophie asked of Anna when they were back in their seats.

Anna pointed to the middle of her back and whispered, "My mother has to braid it for me."

Sophie thought how good that would feel, someone parting your hair and carefully separating the three pieces for each braid.

The first time Sophie was allowed to spend the night with Anna, her mother who had a strong Norwegian accent said, "Welcome, welcome," but it sounded like "Velcome, velcome."

Sophie was struck by the perfect order of the house. The curtains were white and crisscrossed.

Warm kringle was on the counter. The golden strips were the color of Anna's hair, and shiny as if they had been egg washed. Anna immediately shook the cream that had risen to the top of the milk bottle and poured them each a full glass.

They sat dangling their legs off the back porch because it was still a sunny day. The plate between them had only crumbs left. Their milk was half gone. They each had a ring of milk around their smiling mouths

Sophie said, "I want to see your hair all down."

"Later, when we go to bed. I always sleep with it brushed out."

"Maybe I could brush it this time."

At bedtime, Anna and Sophie each had a bed to themselves. Sophie wandered over to the one she would sleep in to touch the pink velvet. The headboards were a pink, like you see in a peach, barely there but rimming the gold color of the fruit, so subtle you had to touch it and trace with your finger the vein of it, the very pinkest velvet of the peach before biting it. The peach was even more succulent, having run your fingers across the fuzz.

Even the curtains were pink. Anna had a large dresser with a mirror. When Anna opened her drawer for pajamas, Sophie saw how neatly folded everything was. Sophie's cedar chest was messy because she had to dig for her underwear and socks and didn't always put things back. Seeing Anna's neat drawers almost brought her to tears. Anna was very special, she could tell.

Sophie carefully pulled the rubber band off each braid. She undid the blue barrettes that matched her dress and put them with her collection of barrettes and ribbons in a pretty box with little velvet lined sections for each color.

Sophie stood behind Anna as she sat before the mirror. The loosened hair flowed in waves that rippled as Sophie carefully pulled the brush through, the nuance of colors making it seem like a ripened wheat field. The texture was nothing like wheat. Not at all. It slid warmly between Sophie's fingers.

Sophie used her fingers to go up under Anna's hair and make it glide back down. Perhaps it was a waft of Anna's smell. A live, electric, pleasure wakened in Sophie. She felt the warmth of her abdomen against Anna's back. She moved closer and touched Anna's back with her stomach.

Anna turned slowly. Their eyes met, the blue of Anna's were milky and tender, widening. She swung her hair, and it was fluid and out of Sophie's hands. Sophie leaned in and each kissed the lips of the other. "I love you," Anna said.

Sophie was stunned that someone so perfect would love her. "I would die for you," Sophie said, knowing of death all too well.

They made an oath and exchanged blood after scratching their wrists with the fingernail scissors. They drew so little blood it seemed to Sophie it should have been a lot more like from a deeper cut. She'd never made an oath before. She had only heard of it.

Sophie climbed into bed with her faded clown pajamas. She had to touch her belly because the feelings of friendship were so new and the feelings seemed all related to how she felt about Dougie when he came into her room that night.

"Good night Anna. You're my best friend ever."

"You're mine too. For always."

Sophie couldn't help but sniffle.

"Sophie?"

"Yes."

"Why are you crying?"

"Will you promise, Anna?"

"On our oath, I will not tell"

"It was my fault my brothers died. It's a secret no one in our family can tell anyone."

Anna sat up in bed. "Not you Sophie."

"Yes, it was me who made it happen."

Sophie didn't feel confused about love. She felt confused about how to express love. It hurt. She held her hand there against the warmth of herself, and it soothed her, but she cried just the same, very silently into her pillow.

Sophie's times thereafter with Anna seemed without the torturous, predatory images of places that waited to attack her mind, like their faces mashed into the mud, their unseeing eyes, their heavy, wet clothes. Cold and wet those eyes must have felt, like when she touched an eyeball of her father's kill. These thoughts often came at night.

Telling Abe about Anna, the words seemed to roll lightly off her tongue. But for now, she could go no further. She was blocked. Abe finished making his notes then lifted his dark head, "Ready for a shower?"

★★★

A female aide came to be with Sophie when she was allowed her first shower. The hot water rained down her back pelting the curve of her spine. She left her head under its strong pressure, scrubbing the rough patches of hair with the bar of soap provided. Her scalp was tender, and she winced as she soaped her scorched forehead. Having used Steve's razor on her brows, they were left inflamed and sore.

She pulled off the fresh dressing around her toe. She sat on the shower bench and examined its whiteness. She rubbed it, nursing the color back. The gravel she had run through had left an array of small bruises and cuts. She rubbed the arches of her feet, lightly touching the bruised heels, thinking back. She remembered how calmly the patrolman had talked to her. He had had the blanket ready. He was burly and handled her easily. How would he ever know the import of his job well done? When had she scraped her thigh? The scabs had softened and she rubbed them off with the towel.

Her thoughts were confused. She wondered why no one other than the pastor had come to see her. Had she embarrassed them? What happened? The bruises on her arms were less purple, but the fingerprints remained like smudged ink. Scenes came back to her. She remembered the sheet around her and how she had waddled to the police car. She remembered in flashes, like a slide show: the dark, crowded freeway, the doctor, her ecstasy, how it became night and how she was trundled away.

Quiet tears came again. Finally, she remembered slipping on the pavement, scraping her thigh. The tears were as warm as her skin from the hot shower. The memories were a shock and humiliating. How was it she had managed to make yet more painful memories to store and relive?

As she dried herself, she felt the plague of guilt. Old feelings still festering in her mind returned as she became more logical. She dredged up the debris of doubts about her self-worth, the ones that had been dispelled for a short time during her mania, and deposited them on an eroded shore of her belief in herself. Where else to put them? They were still part of her. Her shame saturated to the core. She wondered how she had ever come to believe she was called and chosen by God.

Her swatch of pubic hair had begun to grow back and was prickly. She asked the aide for a razor. "No, no 'sharps'," was the reply She was Hispanic, and her *no's* were not round like Sophie's.

The pink scrubs she brought her were starched and fresh, so tightly pressed they had to be teased apart. Other patients wore street clothes, but she had none. She changed, pulling the cord tightly around her waist, and rejoined Abe. She looked down, seeing the sharp creases that would hold all day.

Abe smiled when she emerged. "You look as if you've been folded."

He rubbed his own closely cropped hair. No bushy Afro for him, he had decided long before.

"I have electric clippers if you want to even out your haircut. I've a good amount of practice, given the fact that we have the same hairdo." Sophie smiled.

Sophie's new slippers were still the same shade of green. Abe and she walked to the garden and sat on the single wrought iron bench. Sophie began to talk again. "I need forgiveness," she said.

Abe leaned forward and folded his hands.

"From whom? For what?"

★★★

Sophie's roommate at Bayside did nothing much except stand with her hands behind her back, looking out on a sparsely used parking lot. The wintering trees were bare. She was heavy, especially about her hips. Her breasts were centered mounds with no support. They reminded Sophie of Mountain Bars. She moved sluggishly and didn't speak to Sophie. Her red hair was bushy. From the back one saw a circle of dark roots flattened and spread where she had lain on the pillow.

Sable was her name.

"Hello Sable."

Sable didn't turn, or say hello, but she stepped to one side and peered out as if someone she knew was coming. Even though she had meant to ignore Sophie, she began to cry softly and her shoulders shuddered.

"It's almost time for Christmas, and I'm not ready. I'll be here until they let me go, and that will be too late to buy something for Brady."

"I'm Sophie. Is Brady your child?"

Sophie associated children with Christmas, how overjoyed or disappointed and sad they could be. Sable turned. Sophie could see she was a young woman. Bruises spread across her cheeks. Sable turned, her back to Sophie once again.

"He's only five, my boy Brady. He won't understand. He just won't understand why I'm not there for Christmas and why he won't get a present from me. Right now, he's in a foster home because I'm here.

His step-father burned his cheek with his cigarette to teach him not to say bad words. We fought, and I called the police. I was still in a rage when they arrived. I had a knife in my hand."

Clearly, she needed to talk to someone, because with very little encouragement except Sophie's silence, Sable continued. Her voice lowered as she mentioned her husband.

"Rusty had been down the street drinking too long. He always comes back crazy. But it never got this bad. We may lose guardianship of Brady. The social worker from the state said the episodes have happened too many times."

She paused, lowering her voice to express an irony, "This never happened in Arizona; they're so busy rustling up Indians to put back on the reservation, they didn't pay much attention to us."

With a little hope, she said, "Brady wants a dump truck, a yellow one. He has it all picked out at K-Mart. If I could just get there."

Dump trucks. Something about toy dump trucks resonated in Sophie's mind. She distracted herself quickly by drawing closer to Sable and touching her shoulder.

Sable became more tearful and turned with a smile of sad envy, as if she had a sense of the inequity of her loneliness and sorrow compared with Sophie's.

If she wanted pity, Sophie didn't sense it. Sophie was sympathetic, especially to the five-year-old. She often responded by giving; it relieved her anxieties, compensating for a need she hadn't named.

Feeling compassion for someone else sparked Sophie's hope for herself. She was beginning to understand something about herself in Sable's reflection: Their situations didn't compare.

Sophie would be stronger for this experience whether she regained Steve's respect and affections or not. She had no children to lose, no life really that she cared about losing. The overwhelming need for God she had been so desperate for was now as absent as the aspiration had been present. A great load had lifted.

"It's been hell."

Sable's pain reminded Sophie of Anna's face when she'd visited at Saint Mary's Cancer Center. Both had expressed many complex layers of feelings, which spoke of the solitude of the journey each woman was on.

A welcoming but defeated smile always played about Anna's mouth, and there was more courage in her countenance than Sophie saw in Sable. Anna had never been mistreated. Sable was exhausted, battered and trapped. There was a child.

Sable woke in the middle of that first night; she yelled loudly in the partially-lit room, and it sounded like the yelp of an injured dog. Sophie woke and went to her bedside across the room, talking, soothing saying, "It's okay, Sable, it was just a dream," she said as she knelt beside the bed.

Almost immediately, Sable's night nurse, Frances, came in. Sable looked to both faces, as if foundering after a fall. Sophie took her hand and helped her sit upright.

"Sophie, you can go back to your bed."

Sophie hesitated.

Frances switched on the ceiling light, and for a moment, Sophie looked Sable full face, and saw the cowering, frightened look of despair. Her distress was written full in her distorted features. Her large body shook.

Frances checked Sable's armband, and poured out some water and handed Sable the paper cup that contained her medication.

"Sophie, please get back in bed."

Sable continued to hold her hand in her grip. Sophie used her other hand to loosen it, but Sable leaned toward her, desperately reaching. Sophie understood her in that moment. She, too, had dreams that escaped so quickly all she was left with was desperate guilt and loneliness. Those feelings stretched out into infinity, and ridding herself of them felt as hopeless as banishing the swirling angry clouds.

When Frances finally turned out the light, the nightlight beside the table between them feebly lit Sable's expression of defeat.

"What is it Sable?"

"They're taking Brady," She said in a small voice. "They're taking Brady away from me."

The news had come to her that day from Social Services that she was being transferred to a county facility. Medicaid wouldn't pay the bill for a private hospital. In the meantime, Brady would be placed in long-term foster care. They told her Brady had to remain indefinitely until it was proven Sable could manage.

Sable had hoped she would be released immediately. Unfortunately, that was not to be and a special arranged visit on Christmas Eve would be the last she'd see of him until the court settled on a different arrangement.

Sophie, too, was afraid of where her reality would take her. When she had hallucinated, she had become the very child of God, forgiven and brought into hysteria of worship. Now, as her sanity returned with each day, she relinquished the hope of that kind of joy, indeed any kind of communion and safety with God. Instead there was an absence of joy.

She returned to Sable's bedside like a shadow, slowly caressing her arm, from the meaty part to the forearm, back and forth. She had no truth to share. Finally, the drugs took Sable away, but Sophie stayed to be sure she was in a safe place.

Sable's face became placid; her mouth was slightly open; she was breathing steadily and effortlessly.

Sophie's own breathing became easier. She returned to her bed, but she didn't sleep. The sun broke through the slatted blinds. She heard the hustling of the new shift coming on. She dressed expecting Abe and the broad, white smile that brightened her mornings. What piece of her story would they write today?

★★★

At first, Sophie stayed on clear liquids. The first time she saw the abundance and variety of food in the cafeteria, she looked to Abe as if she didn't know what to make of it or where to start. It was the evening after Sable had woken her in the night.

Suddenly, a young disheveled man jumped up shouting, "Get out of here. Now! I said, Get out of here."

The dining room went quiet. He thrashed about, evidently trying to warn everyone around him of an impending tragedy. He flailed his arms. Two large male orderlies surrounded him in seconds and walked him out. He stumbled forward with his arms behind him.

"I tell you," he turned his head back and shouted, "There's danger here."

Brought up short, Sophie remembered she was in a sanitarium. Silence resettled. Only the shifting of chairs could be heard.

"Can something be done for him?" Sophie said. She felt a chill, as if something evil had left the room.

"There's nothing you or I can do." Abe said.

"Frances told me about Sable's nightmare. She also said that when she checked, you didn't sleep. What kept you awake? Let's focus on finishing your story and getting you back home."

Sophie had difficulty with the concept of home. Right now, here with Abe seemed most like home.

Turning away from the spectacle of the shouting inmate, Abe looked at her plate and said, "We'll take it easy this first time. It's been quite a while since you've had anything but liquids. I'm glad the nausea has passed and the tests are over."

His plate filled as quickly as hers. He took two of the soft rolls and was filling them with meatloaf. He liked catsup, she saw. His appetite amused her. She had expected him to be more choosey.

"When do you have time to work all that off," she smiled.

"I go to a gym, straight from work," he said.

Sophie still felt a bit queasy even though she was also very hungry. They had pulled the feeding tube, and she could feel the puckering skin when she rubbed her stomach in anticipation. She was no longer attached to the IV pole with its bag of crystalloids, dripping drop by measured drop into her vein.

The medication for her psychosis had destabilized her balance, and she felt dizzy. It was hard to focus her eyes. But she knew where she was and something of where she had been. Abe was easy to be with, even though he was gently insistent she go back to her story.

From this point in time, it was difficult to know who'd been culpable of what while she learned to navigate the memories of her childhood world. She recalled those years, and blamed herself, just as she had as a child. She would try telling him what she recalled of her earliest memories.

Before she did, she piled mashed potatoes and the thick slices of meatloaf on her plate. She had never really liked meatloaf, but her stomach was ravenous. Abe stepped back in front of the vegetables as if to signal her, and she went back and took a portion of broccoli and carrots. He stepped back again. She took romaine lettuce with tomatoes and green peppers. There were slices of breaded, sautéed eggplant and she took some of those as well. Her plate was full.

"Go easy." He said again, "let's keep it balanced," "We're resetting your metabolism."

Abe sat with her, and they ate together as if she were being chaperoned. Even her diet mattered to him.

"Annie, the nurse coming on will be with you again through the night. No one has asked permission but if you have visitors after I leave, the doctor on duty and Annie will give them permission or not. If you want to see someone, she'll go with you until the double doors. A different orderly will be in the lobby waiting to be with you. You won't be alone."

"Will you be here tomorrow?"

"When the staff assigns us a new patient, only one, we have them for five days a week. I'll be with you every day this week and until you go. I'll have you as my only patient until you leave. Except that I'm off on the weekends."

Sophie sat up.

"Really? Every day?"

"It's Monday. You came in on Thursday afternoon. Do you know the month?" Abe said.

"December," she said.

"December tenth."

"That's right. It's December tenth."

"How long will I be here? She said.

"The doctor whom you'll see tomorrow will release you when he believes you're ready. Is it clear what happened to you? You *are* liking food again, I can see that."

They chuckled. She had been optimistic about what she could eat and now she pushed her plate away, crossing the plastic knife and fork as if signaling a waiter that she was done. Sable sat across the room, her head in her hands. The nurse held Sable's arm as if to pull her hands away. She pushed the plate closer to Sable, but Sable didn't eat.

"Sable wants a dump truck for her son, Brady. It's very important to her."

★★★

Before Abe obtained his Master's degree in Sociology when he still worked as an RN on an orthopedic floor of the hospital, his wife died suddenly of a heart attack. On the day of her funeral, he had stood looking down into her coffin, a simple box containing his companion of over twenty years. There were no children. He lived alone. He struggled before he set new goals for himself.

One day, coming from the edge of her grave site, new determination rose within him, and he put his mending self doubly into his job and education. He became very effective. He had learned to detach from his patients when they left his care and tolerated the loss of his investment in them.

Abe had seen patients come to terms with death; he had seen the strength it took to accept that uneasy relationship with the inner certainty of an end coming, imagining not being, while knowing the world went on and on.

He had witnessed healing, slow methodical healing, when patients began to recover and come to terms with reality and live out their lives with grace.

Sophie's healing began with his respect. She was his patient, but a person first. Sophie was lucky to have him.

Sophie had experienced death in brutal fashion. In a terrible way, it gave her a foothold. She wouldn't be governed by ignorance; she had encountered death. She could understand herself better. .

After all, the earth claims everything for itself and makes ashes, ashes and ashes of ashes. Whether we're lain in a sarcophagus, tamped down in forest beds or strewn across the earth as dust, we become one with the earth. It's a matter of time.

All ride in the same carriage. As it makes its stops, one knows one's turn will come to shamble off, willing or not. But before then, each day is lived as if it will never end. Find beauty, do it purposefully. What choice is there?

Abe believed her acceptance of death was an important part of healing. He knew, having been rescued from the brink himself. It would certainly be easier than the waiting that Sophie and Anna were doing in the face of her cancer. Sophie would have to acknowledge the resentment and anger that she was carrying too.

Death can be easier than what precedes it.

We seal our loved ones in steel boxes as if to prevent the unavoidable process of rotting under the earth; we shawl the coffins with ribbons and flowers; we blanket the graves with lilies and roses, pretending, distracting, smothering our sorrow. What had Sophie buried so carefully?

★★★

Later Abe said, "Your father is on his way again. Where are your parents from?"

"They have a winter cabin in eastern Washington. That's where they'll be."

"Perhaps you want to see him before anyone else."

"I think I do."

Her father's approach would be an important event in her healing. Abe jotted down the last of his notes from the day. The memories were cobbled together. He would have to sort it out chronologically.

Her affect was no longer so flat. Her countenance had lifted. She had emerged from the mania and then from the shock of understanding. Now she was doing her best to find her way back to the past. She was on her way and engaging in an important dialogue with him.

Elochoman Valley Road, Washington
1949

Their father slammed his fist down on the table. The porcelain jug of milk pitched then righted itself, not spilling. They were seated in their places, napkins already unfolded. The children sat up more straightly. Their mother, Dorothy, was at the stove browning flour in the fat rendered from the venison steak. Steam lifted from the iron skillet as she turned toward the table. The oil cloth had begun to wear, and she noticed the thread-bare spot before she turned to his reddened face. She continued stirring with a fork, and swirled in the milk. The gravy bubbled, and the color evened. They never had a meal without gravy, or it wasn't a meal, Ben said.

The issue was the hammer. It was assumed that the boys had left it in the mud. But Sophie had hidden the hammer, thinking her father wouldn't be able to work on building the garage that evening as was his habit. Then the two of them could play checkers. He was the only one who would play with her. He was the black, and she was red. She was learning to set things up to double jump. He didn't let her win, but sometimes she did anyway, whereupon her elation made her skip around the room.

To hide the hammer, she used the plank laid out into the large bog in the backyard where her brothers watched for frogs. It facilitated Sophie getting out to the middle to throw the hammer in. She had watched it sink and disappear. The plank squished further into the mud with her weight, but she was able to throw the hammer quickly and run back without getting her shoes wet.

Sophie sat to her father's right. She fidgeted and resettled. She righted the silverware. Then she put her hands back in her lap. Nothing good could come of his anger. There was no one to tell on her, because no one had seen her. Obviously the boys had lost the hammer. Ben believed they were the culprits.

Her older brothers would be whipped with a branch they'd first have to cut for themselves. But first, they finished their plates because it took hard earned money to put food on the table. The canned, cream corn slid into Sophie's mound of mashed potatoes. She liked it that way, but she was having trouble swallowing.

The willow switches were cut after dark from the brush alongside the house. After being approved as strong enough by Ben, the whipping took place in the unfinished garage. Matthew looked over to Doug, but Doug looked straight up to the beams.

Doug was oldest of the boys. They came back in, not crying or having said a word. Matthew followed Doug's example. They had looked to the rafters, swallowed hard and bridged their tears, while Punky paced and whined around them during the licking.

Nor would they brood. It wasn't allowed. Mathew's nose dripped. He slid his flannel sleeve across his face as he came back in the house. Punky stood at the door until it shut him outside. Dorothy wouldn't have an inside dog.

Punky was accustomed to waiting at the door. He slept nearby slightly under the house. If the door opened, he was in front of the door wagging his tail. If they left in the car, he walked with them to the car and waited in the drive until they returned. If someone came, he barked once as if to announce them. He sniffed about their tires and waited again at the front door, lying in his customary waiting spot where an old kitchen rug had been laid.

While they were being whipped, Marie, the oldest and most often in charge of the four of the children when Ben and Dorothy went into town, went to her room. She took her doll from the drawer and toyed with the lace. She changed the doll into nightclothes. She listened. It was over. "I promise never to spank you," she said to the doll in her arms. She could be so lofty, but not with her doll.

Sophie had watched the whipping from the window of the soon-to-be-finished bathroom, another home improvement project of her father's. She stood on the unconnected stool as to see. Their father's tools were not to be meddled with. They were tools not playthings, and she should have known. She cried to see them whipped. But she didn't confess, not even when they took her punishment.

The hammer was so worn from use that it had shaped to his large hand, still shiny above and below where he gripped it. Sophie loved the pattern of sound when he pounded a nail: tap; tap tap; tap tap tap; driving it home. She wondered why he didn't take from the boys' earnings selling blackberries to replace the hammer now water-soaked. The mystery of its disappearance bothered Ben. He hadn't gotten to the bottom of it, even with the whipping. Sophie felt sorry she had done it, but she didn't repent.

Sophie, at five, observed her world more than she interacted with it. Her father was her refuge, and she depended upon being an important help to him for her sense of worth. He worked so hard all alone. Building their house from scratch hadn't been easy, especially since they had moved away from the CCC Camp before the addition was completed. It was always being worked on their mother, Dorothy, said and he never would be finished. "He doesn't get a day of rest. Look at this mess of sawdust we live in."

Working on the house or like now the garage, went on in the evening after he returned from his job as a lineman. He had worked his way up to being foreman. Sophie was proud and told people in her Sunday School class he was the boss of the PUD, the Public Utilities District for Wahkiakum County. Having a job was so important, and he was happy in it. He'd been taught by the best Ben said. Mr. Dickson, the manager, who wore a suit to his office, gave him another raise. He also received double time if he had to go on a call after hours.

There was no phone to answer for the PUD after business hours. When someone had a problem after hours, the call was shunted automatically by the local operator to Ben's house phone. If more than one call came in about the same outage, Elsie, the operator at the switchboard, would tell the customer it was already being taken care of. Otherwise, when the phone would ring in the middle of the night, it was most often Dorothy who answered each caller. She then used the radio to contact Ben. She would remark how she should be paid as well.

The PUD was still installing power lines, having recently hooked into Bonneville Power, one of the hydroelectric dams on the Columbia River which gave them the capacity to expand throughout the county. Her father believed the men were being overworked, what with having to set poles and string wire to outlying areas, and being called out at all hours of the night. There were still many outages; yet, people had become accustomed to having power for heat and cooking. The dairies, which had switched to modern milking machines, counted on having power. Demands grew.

Ben usually woke Matthew or Douglas to go with him when a transformer blew or some other outage occurred. Sophie begged and begged to go with him when he was called out. Finally he took her.

Without saying a word, he handed her a square lantern, brighter and more focusable than any ordinary flashlight. She held it on him as he leaned forward and moved the belt wrapped around him and the pole up swiftly and pulled it back, using his caulk boots to grip the pole as he climbed. The pole was old and did not reflect the light well, but it caught her father's face and safety hat.

Her wrists began to ache, but she held the square lamp more tightly, tilting it at just the right angle. All she could see were his gloved hands working in the strong shaft of the light she held. When they drove home, he removed his leather gloves and put them on her lap. He smiled, and as she did every time, she felt herself melt. She believed he smiled at her more often than anyone else. She believed she was his favorite, even if he rarely let on. She slipped the gloves over her hands and felt the warmth inside them. The truck's heater ran full blast

Each evening that he came home to work on the garage Sophie worked alongside him in all of his undertakings. Though she never hid his hammer again, she often wanted him to stop in time for a game. Dorothy made cocoa fudge and brought it to the garage from time to time. Sophie smelled it while it boiled down, anticipating its sweetness.

Inside the house, everything was finished except hooking up the plumbing. The white shale-like siding on the house had proved to be fragile and stretched his patience when he put it up. The edges were sharp and had torn her hands as she lifted them to him. Sometimes he threw a perfectly good one to the ground, if it didn't go in just right. If it didn't break, Sophie put it back on the stack and handed him another.

"Stand back a little Soph," he might say when she held it in the air too soon.

Now, building the garage, Sophie handed him each nail and listened for the last three strong strokes of his hammer before handing him another. The tap of the hammer was sure-handed. They worked together without words. On the ladder Ben turned to her and handed her another handful of nails from his apron, and she held them, offering each shiny six-penny nail back to him one at a time. He would take the one in his mouth and reach with his other hand to accept another.

The lumber was smooth to touch, and he often ran his broad hand against the grain. She did the same as if the smoothness were important. It filled her senses, as did the fragrance when it was cut into, like a melon will open its smell to the kitchen. He would *tssk* if the board they were cutting was warped; slip his hammer into place on his apron, and toss the board on the stack of rejects.

She sometimes foresaw his needs, and she delivered the fat red carpenter pencil, the handsaw, the plane, the level or even the plum bob before he could ask. She also threw the ends of the sawn boards into a salvage pile that continued to grow. She stacked them neatly later.

If the bubble in the level didn't jiggle and settle between the fine lines of the center, they repeated the process of planing and measuring, exchanging a glance and maybe grinning when the bubble was well seated. In that role, Sophie was confident she was useful and needed. Those smiles were her rewards. Although he never acknowledged her verbally, she felt loved and safe beside him.

On the evening of the lost hammer, she had swept the sawdust in the garage into a small heap, tapping the broom against the cement floor. She swept the shreds of the sticks he had used on the boys. The dustpan had a fine, smooth edge on it, and she was able to get it all up with ease. She shuddered at what it would be like for him to be angry with her.

She took pride in the still damp-looking dark cement. She had lugged half-buckets of water to the churning mixer when they poured the sludgy wet concoction over sand and pea gravel on a Saturday when he wasn't on-call and could be sure to finish the job. Her brothers were strong enough to carry full buckets. She ignored the taunts her father couldn't hear over the gravel slushing in the rolling cement mixer. They slid boards back and forth to even it out. They had worried they might have a hard rain before it cured and set. She learned to worry about what he worried over.

Ben had called her and placed her hand into the cold cement. Punky, slipped between them, sniffing. Punky's front paw was also introduced to the cement while her father held him around his body. If you go there, the impressions hold until this day and you'll see how little the hand was that helped make it. There are small pits where Punky's toes punctured the drying cement.

As they knelt, Ben drew Sophie near him, his great arm around her shoulder and pushed the hair away from her face.

She never suffered her father's anger. She did much to please him and navigated carefully around his temper throughout her early childhood. That's why she didn't tell on the boys every time. They often blamed her for being whipped, as it was.

★★★

At Bay Sanitarium where she was telling her story to Abe, it was arranged she see the doctor as part the protocol of her path to wellness. The psychiatrist, Dr. Savoire, was seated when she walked into his small office. It looked out on the stone pathways in the garden. She noted again as she looked out that the ivy around the paths encroached on them, making it necessary to walk single file. The walls of the garden were high. She sensed the reality of being confined. He didn't swivel his chair toward her or acknowledge her arrival at all until she sat in the chair provided for patients.

She had always imagined psychiatrists had luxurious offices. His was spare and colorless just like him. He didn't stand to greet her. From this perspective the view of the garden reminded her that she was alone. She was alone and locked in. Dr. Savoire was a warden to her in that moment, someone who would trap her there.

Finally, he turned and she noticed that his forehead was narrow, and his hairline had receded to the top of his gray- haired head. His long nose began between high brows and raised a tad in the middle before it sloped sharply to its pointed end.

Dr. Savoire looked at the notes in front of him. "You seem to be doing well. Let's not change anything for the next few days."

"I'm sleepier than I'd like to be. I took a two-hour nap today after lunch." She had woken feeling dull and heavy headed. She believed she could only make progress if she were awake.

"Suppressing psychotic behavior calls for a strong medication like Haloperidol." He cleared his throat.

Clearly, he was uninterested in what went on in her mind, the very organ he was trained to help heal.

She persevered. "But I feel now as if I understand what happened. I know I had a breakdown. I'd like to try being off such a strong dose. I feel so groggy."

Stultified by the drugs, her words were slow in coming. She sensed she wasn't convincing him.

"No, not yet. I'll see you again in five days," he stood, his fingers pressed to the blotter on his desk. He picked the next file from a wire stack and placed hers on the bottom.

Sophie slept again before dinner. That night she had insomnia and couldn't relax enough to even try to sleep. Long-submerged memories of her family came to her in droves, an annoying host of spirits she tried to ignore. Across the room, Sable snored, a consistent purring noise

She lowered the sliding rail, slipped out of the bed and went unnoticed into the darkened hallways. The night nurse had raised the rails as if she were a child.

The patients had been put to bed long before. Barefoot, she walked the hallways, gripping the smooth rail that had fascinated her the first day when she became conscious. The garden was not even subtly lit. She shielded her eyes, trying to see out.

She saw her father's disgust as he spit between his teeth. She covered her face in defense as if to close out the images, to stop the movement of memories through her mind. The thoughts were like children chained together hand in hand circling her with cruel taunts.

She stepped back from the cold glass partition with a shiver. She was turned around and couldn't find her door from among the others. Somewhere in one of the hallways was her room. She didn't remember the number. She felt the panic of being alone with only her memories which would not retreat. There was a dark swirling pond, gurgling over a dam that was black as pitch. She saw a twisted leg, a leather boot oozing mud. The images were more and more vivid, and relentless. Her heart rebelled at the onslaught.

She went to the end of one of the halls to the nurses' station. No one appeared, and she rang a chrome finished bell. The ding sounded like the bell on one of her brothers' bikes. She jumped at the memory. The bike was candy-apple red. After what had happened, it stayed in the garage for years, its tires deflated, its pedals rusting. No one owned it anymore. It went from being cherished, waxed and polished into disuse in the course of a moment.

Seeing her up and about, the secretary called the nurse on duty. Paula was tall, her hair dyed to a deep unnatural black. Sophie's grandmother had dyed her hair at home, and you could see the black on her scalp when she first did it. Paula's had been done at home too, Sophie noted.

"Dear, dear, dear, you should be in bed. Where are your slippers? Here, let me tie your gown in the back. Where are your slippers?"

"I couldn't sleep, and now I'm lost." The memories were in disorder and would not come in sequence. The lights were dimmed and Sophie hated the dark. Sophie saw the large clock above the secretary's head. It read 2:00 am, the darkest time.

Leading her down the hallway to room 208, Paula said, "We must not wake your room mate."

"I'll try not to. Bless her heart; she sleeps most of the time. Her name is Sable."

"I know Sable. She'll be leaving in time for Christmas Eve."

Sophie wanted her to have a yellow dump truck from K-Mart by then. It was metal and small; she could imagine it in her hand, pulling the little lever. Every tiny detail filled itself in whether she wanted it to or not. The valley of memories she walks through darkens. She takes the opportune medication they hand her, glad for it to bring back the night. Sleep, sleep. She wanted sleep.

★★★

After breakfast with Abe, Sophie talked with Joanie, another inmate. She handled the doll Joanie carried carefully when Joanie passed it over to her. She folded the worn flannel around its painted but smeared toes. The rubber was stained from removing and replacing the polish. Joanie explained she couldn't use polish in the hospital and apologized that the little toes weren't as perfect as usual.

Sophie thought back to her one and only doll. Amosandra hadn't been fancy either. Sophie had to hide her to keep her safe. She handed Joanie's back to her.

Joanie's own nails resembled Sophie's. Joanie bothered hers while the pretend baby slept. Joanie leaned her head on Sophie's shoulder. Sophie looked to Abe, and he nodded that it was okay even though the rules didn't allow touching among the patients.

Abe had the advantage of his years of experience, his degrees in psychology and training as an RN. His curiosity was that rare and genuine need to know and understand how the fragile patients of a psych ward could each be shown their way forward.

He was also aware of what it felt like to court oblivion.

When he put Sara in the grave, he went home and turned his face to the wall and cried like a baby. The pills were there. He had handled the bottle, reading the date as he spilled them into his hand and counted them. He might have used them, but Old Man Cooper had come by and quite literally kicked him.

"Get out of that bed, or you'll die there."

There were tears in the old man's dark eyes, and they coursed crookedly down his grizzled cheeks. "Elbert told me you were here, like you were dying. No food in the house. Get up, man, and put these flowers I brought on that grave."

He stuffed the flowers in the sink and plugged the drain. The faucet, opened full blast, covered the stems of the Chrysanthemums. They slipped down and floated face first in the cold water.

Cooper opened the bag he brought, split three wieners down the middle and fried them in a cast iron skillet until they were dark around the edges. He pulled out the Gulden's mustard. Abe ate.

"Nothing going to bring her back, Abe."

Abe rescued the flowers and disentangled the ferns poked among them. He washed a cloudy vase and arranged them in the fashion in which he would place them on Sara's grave.

★★★

Abe thought in those few days that the edges between Sophie's beliefs and her doubts had softened and blurred. She understood now that she had lost her mind for a time. She was able to accept it without a great deal of stress. She would not have to trawl towing this embarrassment behind her, which might well have dragged her to the bottom.

Instead, she came to know that there was no longer any battle for her sanity. There was a gentler, quieter way back to her life. She was disarmed and submitted, finally, to the memories that came. They poured out of her as she talked with Abe.

How would Steve, the aspiring minister, accept her insanity? Would the parishioners malign him? In the context of their fundamental beliefs, would not those in the congregation associate it with Satan, God of the demonic realm? The stigmatism might be too much for the young minister. Abe wondered about Sophie, how the person he was coming to know would abide Steve's domineering presence. He had begun to believe a separation from Steve might be a healthy decision on Sophie's part.

Sophie, by contrast realized how uneasy she had always been with Steve. With Abe, she had the ease of knowing she wasn't being judged. She no longer felt the need for Steve's approval.

She was not special to God; she was simply human. Her compassion was heightened but in a healthy way that came from her strength to give it. She felt committed to salvaging herself from the spoils of her insanity, though it was a different self.

Sophie talked and talked to Abe of the ugly pattern of her days when her father wasn't present, as if one subject led to the other. She was the baby.

At five, her brothers still called her the baby. The worst was how Matthew and Doug treated her when no one was looking. Eventually she had come to know that if she told her parents of the things they did, even those things like going to the forbidden lake, or cutting down a tree, no one would be happy ever. They would be in trouble, and therefore she would be in trouble with them.

★★★

Elochoman Valley Road, 1949

One day, her brothers pulled a ladder up against the house and climbed on the roof. They put their hands to their brows as if they were scouting.

"Do you want to come up?" Doug offered.

Sophie very much wanted to join their fun. She climbed up, scared but brave, and while she stood looking across the way toward Mr. Weidisaari's property, they scrambled down and pulled the ladder away.

It was Monday, wash day, and Dorothy was busy sorting the darks from the lights. The water was steaming and the noisy Electrolux was swishing the clothes back and forth. Finally her mother heard her calling when she went out doors to the clothes line. She had shut the agitator off and circled trying to find her. Sophie was embarrassed and knew she should have known better than to climb on the roof to join her brothers.

Her mother found her there alone near the eave trough, uncomfortable on the pebbly asphalt roofing. She was picking at the tarpaper, and pitch got on her hands.

Dorothy resettled the ladder for her. "It shouldn't be out here in the first place."

It was wooden and heavy. Sophie held the narrowest end as they carried it back to its place.

She tried to help her mother hang clothes. But the tar on her hands stained the first towel she picked up.

"How will I ever get that out? It's ruined." Dorothy said, throwing it down.

"Go wash," she demanded, and just like that Sophie was dismissed.

Sophie knew about these things: pitch, tar, anything like that was hard to get off even if you used Lava soap. She found the red gas can in the garage and poured some over her hand. Some splashed onto her dress. Finally, with the help of a grease rag, it came off. She reeked of gas.

She returned to stand near the wringer machine as her mother worked. Sophie pulled her hands through the tub with the bluing in it, the perfectly clear, blue, rinse water, pretending it was a blue ocean. She saw the bottle in her mind's eye, on the shelf with the bar of Fels-Naptha soap which had been grated into the wash tub. Once, Matthew and Doug had made the frog pond sudsy and colored it blue, getting into big trouble.

Sophie liked catching the flattened clothes coming through the wringer, then watching them unfurl in the blue water, like parachutes full of air.

She had changed her dress and put the ruined hand-me-down in the burn barrel. Her mother didn't notice.

"How in the world did you get up there?" Dorothy asked. "You should have known better."

"The ladder fell when I started to come down." Sophie said.

"That's a likely story," Dorothy said.

"Just wait until your father gets home," she later told the boys.

★★★

"Tattle tale," they said to Sophie.

But she hadn't told at all. She'd lied for them. Still it ended the same way. When she tattled, it changed the atmosphere of the whole family. Things became dark and somber. When she didn't, she found herself in trouble. Every other little situation seemed to necessitate a lie, or the breaking of a promise, one way or the other.

"You're always telling on them," Marie said. "You're a trouble-maker."

"They take Punky across the road, and they're not supposed to." Sophie said.

"What they do is none of your business," her know-it-all sister said.

"But Punky …"

Punky, the bird dog, a beautiful Springer Spaniel, belonged to her brothers, but she loved him too. When he wasn't off with them, they would sit together on the front steps. She kept her hand on his warm back, buried in his black fur.

Still, she tagged after her brothers wanting to be included in their play. She had given up being with Marie long ago. Her only time with her was when they read in the evenings.

One day when the boys were cutting wood for the fireplace with Ben, Sophie taught herself to ride on Doug's red bike, having to swing her leg around the seat to miss the bar. It was a deep metallic red with flecks of silver. She skinned her knee when she rammed into the corner of the house and bruised herself between her legs. The fragile siding of the house cracked apart. She quickly picked up the fragments and took them to the burn barrel. She shoved the pieces beneath the empty vegetable cans. How it happened remained a mystery to the family. The lie was like acid in her throat, but it was the safest way.

There never was a pink bike for her like she wanted. Only the boys got bikes. The Valley Road was too dangerous for her to ride on, they all said.

She often sat quietly fascinated with her sores and picked at them. Recently, she had scraped her arm on a board she was handling, and the scab was striped and long. She could rip each little strip off in one pull, just when it had whitened around the edges. There would be a tiny trail of blood. She sucked it off.

She fantasized while she sat carefully detaching the crust of a sore. She was a concert pianist; she was a dancer. She rode beautiful horses like Black Beauty. She married someone very wealthy, and they rode in a Cadillac in a big city where you could window-shop all day. These were her secret times. She often sat in the new bathroom contemplating all these things until someone needed to go.

She had Marie's old paper dolls. The tabs to hold the clothes on were worn and wouldn't hold the dress onto the shoulders. Sophie Scotch-taped all the tabs, but then she couldn't undress them again.

"I just gave those to you. Now, they're ruined," Marie said, before she wadded up the whole bunch.

Sophie followed her to the burn barrel, but the damage was too great to retrieve them after Marie put them in face first.

★★★

One afternoon, against their father's rule, Sophie followed the boys into the old orchard. Many of the scarred up branches were low enough for her to climb. But the boys climbed higher and threw the un-ripened fruit at her like bullets. At first she thought they wanted her to catch them. She retreated once she saw they were throwing them overhand like a hard ball.

"You can't come up; don't come any higher."

Wandering to the ditch, she scooped a handful of tadpoles from the trench alongside Elochoman Valley Road where they lived. She was watching them swim in her hands when they found her. Matthew forced her hands to put them back.

"Those are going to be frogs; you don't even know, do you?" Doug said.

"Frogs come from eggs, just like babies do," Matthew said.

"Chicken eggs?"

"No dummy, I bet you didn't know Mama has eggs, and Daddy makes it happen so they turn into babies in her stomach. These are just babies, like you. You're the baby. Baby, baby, baby. We should call you Polly Wog; you baby."

Doug seemed to know all about things like that. They had sources of information she didn't. Marie had taught her to read, but there was nothing she could find about the house that told how babies came to be. That did not become clear until later when she read her sister's books. Sometimes the books were returned to the library before she finished them. Dougie never told her how it happened. If he had, she would have been even more scared the night he came in her room.

Matthew and Douglas were given BB guns. Sophie unintentionally made trouble. First of all, she unknowingly stood in the shooting range (that was, in fact, the whole yard).

"Get out of the way," they said. "Girls don't even get to have guns, and you're just in the way."

They made targets of cardboard and nailed them to the trees, even though you should never put a nail in a tree. By taking up the whole front yard they could both practice at the same time. Matthew's target, which he missed completely, pointed across the road toward Mr. Weidisaari's house.

The sound of the window breaking had a nice sharp whack to it followed by the sound of tinkling glass. Sophie ran in and told her mother who called the PUD. Arriving home in his work truck, Ben took the BB guns and broke them over his knee. He spit on the ground and left to return to work without a word.

Mr Weidisaari lived across the road in a small, dark log cabin, a hermit, whom Sophie had never met, only seen. He was a fisherman and went out for days at a time on his gill-netter. The cabin was always dark because he had no electricity. Thick brush grew up around the one room house, and wrapped around the windows like wreaths.

One could tell when he was home by the narrow sleeve of smoke from his wood burning stove. In the evenings, he used a kerosene lamp to repair his nets, and they watched to see the flicker of it move from one corner of the room to the corner where he kept his bed.

Knowing he had a .22 rifle, they stayed away when he was home. Ben whipped them both with his leather belt that evening, and Sophie watched them in the garage from the stool in the bathroom. Doug didn't tell that it was Matthew who had shot out the window.

Subsequently, the brothers made sling shots and aimed at the crows that bounced among the mud puddles on the gravel driveway. They shot toward the power lines. They shot at the clean white sheets hanging to dry. They examined the wings and the beak of a Blue Jay they'd shot, but wouldn't show her. She always remembered its mouth stretched open.

They threw rocks at their orange cat so that it skedaddled across the dandelions and into the brush. No one fed the cat, but she had her litter in the old lopsided buggy. She was almost a pet. Sophie claimed one of the kittens and had begun to tame it, secreting food to it until it could hunt. The other kittens were feral and hissed at them. Except Marie, the children fussed over them as they mewed and hissed. They tried to make friends until they all disappeared one day, including the one she had almost tamed.

Dorothy said, "Sometimes the mother will carry them off like that to a hiding place."

★★★

Once, Doug and Matthew tried starting fires by rubbing sticks together. When that failed they resorted to matches for the miniature bonfire they made of twigs beneath the cedar.

"You shouldn't play with matches or you'll get into trouble," Sophie said.

"Not unless you tell, tattle tale. Leave us alone."

Girls didn't have the privileges that boys had. Doug's heart went out to Sophie, though he rarely made it easier for her. She wanted everything to be right, he thought, but she didn't know the limitations of just being a girl. She wouldn't understand she's the baby.

Beneath the large cedar in the yard, among the tangled, exposed roots, the brothers had created a miniature world. Roads circled around the tree with over passes and tunnels beneath the arching roots. To Sophie it was a magical place. She watched them, even though she wasn't welcome.

Once, when they went out on their bikes, she got bored of reading. She had read all of the Nancy Drew books loaned to her several times. She had determined to read the Bible, but when she got to the long chapters of who begat whom, she lost interest. Genesis and Exodus were okay.

The boys had gone as far as the Moore's where they could pet the work horses through the fence. She had enough time to sneak beneath the tree and play in the miniature world there. She knelt down and filled the yellow dump truck with gravel from the driveway. She loved playing cars and trucks, but she wondered where the magic went when she played alone and was not supposed to be there according to them. The dump truck was small and of a metal that felt solid in her hand. She had flipped the dirt into the main intersection where the cars most often crashed.

After the thrill of watching the vehicles race and crash, it was impossible to muster the same mood. They would fill-up with gas or drive into a ditch. She stopped imagining how one road might be a logging road or state highway, perhaps 804 along the Columbia on the way to Longview.

She knelt with the yellow truck in her hands, examining the hinges, filling it, tipping it with the small lever so it dumped small piles of dirt on the uneven parts of the road they had excavated. She liked to help, but it didn't make her happy to be in their coveted space.

Skidding their bikes into the driveway, dragging their shoes through the puddles, spitting gravel behind them, they stopped near her as she knelt.

"Get out of there. You're not allowed."

"Tomboy," Matthew said.

Thinking to be a help, she had filled another of the dump trucks with dirt because she meant to widen the intersection so the cars on each side could travel safely. She didn't understand they wanted for them to crash.

"You've ruined the main highway."

"Chicken legs. Why do you have those bumps on your legs? Always wants to play with the boys. You don't even look like a girl. No wonder you want to play trucks," Doug said. "You should wear pants if you want to be a boy so much."

Sophie worried about looking like a boy.

"You're straight as a stick," they said.

Later, she scrutinized herself in the mirror, looking for the double chin they said she had, just like Sister Rose at church, whose wattle sagged and folded into her neck. She stepped onto the toilet seat of the outhouse where a long scratched mirror hung. In the dim light, she smoothed down her hair to see how it would look. She felt for hips but there was not even the beginning of curves. She did, she thought, look just like a boy.

"Why don't you play with dolls like real girls?"

There was no doll. Her mother said she'd never play with it even if she had one. All that Sophie knew about dolls was from watching her older sister play house with her friend, Leota and their dolls.

★★★

Marie was older than Sophie by six years. She wouldn't allow Sophie to touch the beautiful porcelain face of her doll, Carol, ever. Carol's main dress was long and silky. She had other outfits that Leota's mom had made. They were always changing the dolls' clothes or working with their hair. Marie usually kept Carol's blonde hair in ringlets because she went to pretend parties. Marie had a tiny tea set, but Sophie couldn't touch that either. There were roses on it, and they poured each other apple cider to look like tea. Marie wanted tennis clothes for Carol and a pretend racquet.

Leota, Marie's best friend, came often to spend the night or vice versa. When she went for a sleepover at Leota's house on Puget Island, Marie would pack Carol's clothes in a brown plaid hatbox.

When Leota came, since Sophie didn't have her own room or her own bed, she slept in a green canvas sleeping bag on the floor. The green and blue plaid flannel inside was soft. She began to feel as if it were hers. She wasn't allowed in to Marie's room when Leota came. She dragged the canvas sack to her parents' room and lay down near the cedar chest. That's where her clothes were anyway.

Marie's room was the only wallpapered room in the house. Marie had chosen larger-than-life hydrangeas. A hint of purple tinged their edges, and the leaves were a subdued green softer than nature's. Marie had been allowed to choose it.

Sophie wondered how it felt to be the oldest.

The day Dorothy and Marie hung the wall paper, Sophie wasn't allowed to carry the wet rolls from the bathtub or hold it while they rolled it on the wall. Instead, she was told to go play and stay out of the way. The room was being transformed into a garden.

When she returned, the beauty of the room took her breath away. The woodwork in contrasting shining white enamel paint, was still wet, she was warned.

The bed was an old brass bed. They were still polishing it when Sophie returned. Sophie was given a rag to follow Marie and rub off the brass cleaner. The rag was already black from the tarnish. She exchanged it for a fresh one and burnished the brass behind Marie until it shone.

Sophie had an allotted space in the double bed, up to the fourth rail of the bedstead, no further. Being the oldest child was an important position in the family.

Sophie tried to always be of help. She had stopped being outwardly angry at them at a very young age, believing she would be more likely to be included if she acted nonchalant. Anger frightened her. She did not allow herself to act on it, especially toward any of her family members. She was embarrassed at the drop of a hat. While she eventually overcame the painful blushing, she grew to become an introvert, one who smiled but didn't engage, a character that did not come to her naturally. There was no pay off, only pain. She tried desperately to appear indifferent.

She often sat, singing to herself, making up the words as she went.

"Silly noises," her father said. "Stop the silly noises."

There didn't seem like there was any way to just be. Sometimes she pulled out little patches of her hair for no good reason. If you took a small amount, it was rather pleasurable, and her mother wouldn't notice.

"Stop wiggling," Marie said over and over when they were in bed together.

Sophie's mind flew everywhere before she slept; it seemed natural to move. Their mother was always told by Marie how Sophie had wiggled in the night.

"Get to sleep. Marie has school tomorrow." She would stand at the door for a moment and check back later, time and again to keep an eye.

Sophie pretended to be asleep. She could make herself not move, but she couldn't shut off her brain.

She lay on her back perfectly still, pretending to be dead in a gold coffin. She had fantasies about dying, how everyone would cry and be sorry. She had many fantasies about herself, including being like Shirley Temple, dancing and singing about the good ship Lollipop. About being a cripple like Tiny

Tim and everywhere you went people would welcome you and help you so gently.

Sophie was afraid to be alone in the dark. Those nights Marie was at Leota's house she didn't move a muscle unless she got her way about leaving a light on. Sometimes she was allowed. If not, she brought the covers in under her, leaving a breathing hole at the top. She slept in the middle of the bed where the mattress slumped. She really never overcame her fear of the dark. Even a candle could make her feel safe. She sometimes snuck the flashlight into her room and read. She felt to blame when the batteries went dead when it was truly needed, but she continued to read in secret.

One night when Marie was home, Sophie counted to the fourth rail and crawled in. Actually, her sister had tied a pale blue ribbon there and she didn't need to count but she was in the habit now. The bed springs creaked. Marie's bedtime was later. On such a night, lying on her back, Sophie lightly touched her abdomen, and it shuddered like a horse's withers will shudder if you accidentally graze your hand against it or even nearby. It was pleasurable, and she fell asleep with one hand under her stomach. It soothed her and made her less afraid of the dark. The room had to be dark. It was Marie's rule, when she was home.

When it was Marie's bedtime, she discovered Sophie asleep with her hand under her pajamas. Yanking the pillow from beneath her head, she said, "That's nasty."

Then she called out, "Mother, Mother."

Nasty was the worst word Sophie could hear; in fact she had heard it only rarely. Nasty was bad. Dazed, barely awake, she didn't understand what had just happened, but she felt betrayed.

For the first and last time, Sophie was spanked. She hadn't understood at first. It felt like a trick. Marie looked on while their mother smacked Sophie's bare bottom. Sophie felt humiliated bent over her lap.

"This is serious business," her mother said.

"I don't want to sleep with her tonight," Marie said.

Dorothy dragged out the sleeping bag and left it on the floor in Marie's room. "This is the last time this will happen."

Sophie continued touching herself from then on anyway when Marie was away. She'd put a pillow in between her legs sometimes when the urge was there and she couldn't deny exploring that warm and moist secret place. One evening, she instinctively pushed the corner of her pillow in that place. It felt good. She would push the pillow as tight and close as she could and move against it. Why was it she wanted to move?

She never forgot again to remove her hand. She had to be careful Marie never saw. Even though Sophie might be asleep, Marie began switching on the ceiling light each night anyway, just to check.

★★★

Emma, Sophie's paternal grandmother, came to live with them after she quit her job as a pie maker in Portland. She was famous for her fruit pies but she left that year before the fruit came on. She knew she would miss the first pie cherries that came in to be sorted, gliding like jewels through her fingers in the cold water.

The day she came was early in April, when blossoms had begun to promote summer's harvest. Sophie skipped ahead to show her the unfinished, unpainted room that would be hers.

The painful arthritis in Emma's knees had taken away her ability to stand for long periods. She was strong in adversity; she would have preferred living alone. The stairs up to her apartment had become harder. The landlord had raised the rent. She had to stand all day making pies.

Sophie had hoped the little yellow canary, Percy, would have come with her, but Dorothy said birds were messy. "Percy went to a better place," they said.

The only piece of furniture she brought was a walnut vanity that had mirrors on each side that folded out. They looked in the want ads for a bed for her. Nothing matched, but she didn't mind about that.

"I left it all behind a long time ago," she said.

She was eighty. Maybe people become more content when they're old, Sophie thought. Sophie was still five, excited to be six and go to school in the fall. She knew she didn't deserve a room of her own.

Under her grandmother's arms hung layers of loose skin that swung when she moved. She was bent over rubbing her swollen knees with liniment, with Sophie beside her in the kitchen when Sophie was brave enough to touch the draping skin and feel it wobble. Her grandmother looked her straight in the eye and said, "Someday you'll be old."

Things went well enough. The bedroom got finished. They painted it pink to match the new tile in the finished bathroom. Emma disliked pink, and she was grateful the chenille bedspread was pure white. Sophie sometimes picked at the tiny white tufts when they talked of the olden days. Emma's grandmother was killed by the Indians. She told it like it was true.

Sophie had hoped for a room, but she was also excited about having someone who might be on her side when things happened. Grandma watched more than she spoke, and sometimes she winked at Sophie as if they had a secret.

Sophie read to Grandma because her eyesight was going. Sometimes when Sophie read to her in the living room, Emma farted. "Stop that Sophie," she'd say, but they all knew who did it.

The silent ones were the worst.

"Yes, stop that Sophie," Matthew said.

They snickered behind her back, pushing their bottoms out as if to let out gas. They pinched their noses out of sight of their grandmother who knew and found it funny. Life was life.

Sometimes Sophie's shoes got too small or the new ones were too slippery and rubbed her heel. She wore Band Aids but they didn't adhere to the blisters very well. She put on white socks and the blister's pus would make a yellow circle around her heel. There was a big difference between a blister and a scab. Often, the blister dried against the sock, and even then it was very painful to pull it off. She found her grandmother one day looking at the yellow circles on the inside of the heels of her shoes, but nothing was said. At home, she didn't wear the shoes that caused them. She went around in her socks. Sophie sensed her grandmother saw things her mother didn't.

Emma asked to grow a garden. It was, after all, April, when the urge to grow things is like different blood in your veins. All she needed were a few rows out of the side lawn. It was just the season to get started, she said. Ben plowed up space for a garden. "It's so much trouble and ruins the look of the lawn we finally got growing," Dorothy complained.

She didn't like everything changing. "I didn't marry you to be a farmer," she said, when he came off the tractor.

They bought 100 baby chicks and kept them under a heater until they strutted around the yard and grew rusty red feathers instead of cute yellow fuzz.

Sophie, who couldn't imagine a hundred chickens, said as she watched them gather in a batch under the heater, "May I hold one?"

"Chickens aren't pets," Emma said.

But it could have been that one might have been her pet Sophie thought. The widows next door each had a pet chicken that slept near their chairs. The smell was peculiar to their house. Dorothy said it was a dirty way to live.

"It's disgusting, they leave a trail wherever they go," Dorothy said.

"One rooster is enough to serve them all," Grandma said surveying the chicks, her hands on her hips.

Sophie wondered what the rooster would serve.

On a sunny afternoon, Sophie went into the warm chicken house before her father came home and put as many baby chicks as would fit into the wagon. The chicks jumped out and ran away until she filled the wagon with straw. Then they stayed in, and she pulled them out the door around the quickly constructed henhouse, thinking they could use some fresh air. Grandma always talked about needing fresh air.

Again, they began leaping to the ground, one by one. When she bounded after one, another would leap and scuttle away.

"You dummy. They need to be under the light. If they get cold, they'll die." Matthew said.

He held one in the cup of his hands, his cheek against the softness.

Doug took his coat and laid it over the remaining chicks. After they had chased them down and successfully deposited them in the chicken house, the baby chicks swarmed about beneath the warming light. With the door firmly closed behind them, out of earshot, Doug said, "Sophie, it's very important you understand … "

Sometimes Doug was nicer to her though only when they were alone. He returned the wagon to the garage, came back and rested his hands on her shoulders. His kindness and her disappointment that she couldn't take them for a ride made her cry. She hoped that at least one chick would stay a baby. She had poor judgment he told her. They walked in the woods and she sat on his shoulders.

As it turned out, the red Leghorn cock with his red comb and long black hackles grew tall, and roamed about the yard each day stretching his neck. He would turn his head from side to side sharply as if danger lurked everywhere. The hens kept their heads down, pecking the ground in a jerking fashion, always in motion until sundown when they all headed inside to roost until the cock crowed early the next morning. Sophie listened for the insistent sound, and put her feet on the floor, waking her sister way too soon to get up.

By that August, when the hens had grown and began to lay eggs, Grandma was proud to take the wire basket out and gather them. If a hen didn't lay eggs, she killed it. After it flounced and flew around the yard without its head, she doused it in boiling water and plucked it. Her hands covered in wet, clinging red feathers made Sophie shudder.

Then they had it for dinner with Grandma's doughy home-made noodles. Sophie was beginning to get over the idea of animals being killed, and served for dinner, like the back strap of a just-killed buck, still warm to touch when she helped dredge it in the salt and peppered flour.

When Sophie gathered the eggs, she hated putting her hand under a hen to feel for an egg. The little basin of hay was warm. The hen would squawk and be unsettled, and the disturbed straw made it dusty. Her Grandma could get the egg without disturbing the chicken. Sophie tagged after her grandmother. She wanted to learn some of her ways, but the standard was high.

Dorothy's mother-in-law talked her son into many projects once she was ensconced in the house. Although she was quiet, she was forceful. Grandma wanted control. She believed in a woman's rights. Ben was pleased to make her happy, because like back on the prairie, a family should be self-sufficient. It was a thing to be proud of.

About the same time as the baby chicks came, her father took on another such endeavor to build a shed for a cow. Betsy, a young Holstein, was still a heifer. Sophie watched when the veterinarian came and artificially inseminated her. His arm went way into her bottom, and he grinned at her father when he withdrew it.

"Think we did it," he said.

She thought perhaps her father's arm had to plant the egg that had made her a baby inside her mother.

During the summer Emma would bend at the waist to care for the garden, and it seemed to the other children she didn't hear them. Indeed, she acted hard of hearing, but she wasn't. Sophie knew she heard well enough.

"Look how long her boobs are."

"They're enormous," Matthew said.

"Someday you'll get old," Sophie said, quoting Grandma.

"Not like that." Doug said. "She used to be fat. That's why everything hangs. Mama thinks she should wear a corset and keep it altogether." He whispered, "You're too pretty to ever be fat, Soph, you're so pretty."

Sophie took the compliment inside herself, but at the same time she wanted to protect Grandma from the hurtful things they said.

Emma stood up, her arms bracing her back. Her apron was smudged with the black soil. She looked at the boys and spit straight to the ground, just like Ben when he was angry. She always seemed to be fed up with something when the boys were around.

But sometimes she told stories of how her grandmother was absconded by the Caws, a tribe of Native Americans to be feared, she told them. The boys listened up then and sat closer.

"You must hate Indians," Matthew said.

She took Matthew's chin in her hand and said, "Never learn to hate anyone."

"My teacher said it's wrong, what happened to the first to be here Americans." Doug told of his American history class.

When the boys dueled in the living room with her knitting needles she took them back and said, "Don't ever touch my things again or I will tell your father."

That was a warning, they took to heart.

Dorothy hated that the chickens were allowed to peck around the yard. They need calcium Grandma said. She threw out the oyster shells for them. The whiteness in them winked back in the sunlight as the hens hovered over them. The chickens would peck at anything, they were that dumb, Matthew said.

It was October, nearly November, about the time of her birthday when Emma decided she wanted to be baptized in the river, not in the baptismal tank of the Methodist Church in the next town, but in about the coldest river you can come across outside Alaska. The Elochoman River that ran through their valley was melted snow, pure run-off from the surrounding mountains. Cold as ice.

The rills caught the streams; the streams channeled into the creeks, and the creeks diverged into the river; the river caught them in their confluence and cascaded down rocky slopes to spread its cumulative self in the flat land of its self-made valley, slashing open the green earth during the spring rush, exposing rocks of every size, some jagged, disturbing the current in a new way. Some of the small river rocks were made smooth and flattened by the never ending progress of the river to the ocean. Sophie loved the waterfalls spewing from the mountains and often put them in the pictures she drew.

She had a collection of small flat river rocks that she kept in a sock.

Their river poured through the valley with nearly the same strength in the fall and winter as in the summer. Snow on the mountains came and went, quenching the river's lust for water. Finally, it smoothed and flowed into the Columbia, a greater river, and out to the Pacific.

Before she would be baptized, Grandma needed to confess in public. Soon after her announcement she attended a service with the family. She responded to the altar call, a given conclusion to any service. *"Softly and tenderly, Jesus is calling, calling 'Oh sinner come home'."*

Sophie went down to several altar calls, until her father told her that once was enough. She still felt the tug, the tug to really feel. If she had a friend like Jesus she would never feel alone.

The pastor came from behind his pulpit and down to the altar where Emma lowered herself and settled to kneel properly, her crinkly hands steepled at her chin. She had her corset on. Sophie didn't think she looked as flabby as she had out in the garden.

When that was done, the congregation gathered at the river in the valley, and sang about the *"Beautiful, beautiful river straight from the heart of God."* Finally, at the age of eighty, Emma had given her heart to the Carpenter's son, whose goodness reminded her of her son. She had rarely gone to church with Ben and family, but she wanted to make her confession in front of the congregation before she died.

She was the only one to be baptized that day. They rarely baptized in the river anymore anyway, let alone in a cold month. The sun shone, as if condoning her choice and when she slipped into the white robe, she shone, pleased with herself, given her bravery and courage to act out her conversion. Sophie could see she was pleased because she saw the downward movement of her jaw, a rather smug look.

Down she went, suddenly recoiling with a great chill from the water that swept around her. Two shivering elders were there to help the pastor. The current might have taken her otherwise. Here the river swirled and eddied around huge rocks, and the pool that came of it circled upon itself. Everyone applauded when she came back up. She came up the bank and met no one's eye. She had her dignity. Ben wrapped her in blankets.

The act signified a great deal, but did not change her ways. She remained silently critical of her son's wife. She scolded her under her breath about wasting good food. She often messed up the kitchen making a pie or got in the way stirring the rice pudding baking in the oven just when Dorothy was making dinner.

Sophie helped cut the lard into the flour for the pie crust. Grandma taught her how to flute the edges with a not too firm pinch. The mess could get pretty big. Sophie learned you never clean up flour with a wet rag. No, you don't wash the rolling pin either. She taught Sophie things she might not have learned otherwise, little tricks that make a difference.

Sophie was usually only in the kitchen helping when her grandmother was baking bread or making cookies or pies.

For sugar cookies, Sophie learned to cream the butter into the sugar until it was light. The mixture had to be nearly white before adding the eggs with deep yellow yolks, like the yellow Sophie put in her pictures.

Emma also showed Dorothy the way to do things: she tore up old flannel sheets and put them in the linen closet as rags to be used when cleaning. Who needed to buy all these things? Once the cow got going, she churned the cream into butter. She squeezed the water out of it at the kitchen sink. The butter sat out, giving off a near rancid scent, but it was the right consistency to butter toast from the endless loaves of bread she baked. The boys wanted Wonder Bread, but she wouldn't hear of it.

Solutions for the not quite well run home were close at hand. Emma mended and sorted through the laundry to find clothing that needed her healing stitch. She asked for flannel and made all four children new pajamas. They were large on them. They lasted until they were faded.

The prints of cowboys and Indians on the boys' pajamas were like ghosts, the browns and blacks all run together. There were pink Hermosa rosebuds for Marie, and the roses seemed to open with each washing, shot through as they were with a heavy dose of bleach. Sophie's had a pattern of a red nosed clown in a yellow jacket. The nose went pink; the yellow jacket on the clown became a color like mustard. Sophie hated her pajamas. Perhaps she would get store-bought ones for Christmas.

Sophie wanted a pet she could love. The bull calf, once pulled from the cow, had been knocked in the head because it would produce no milk.

"Go in the house Sophie," her father had said.

She had hoped for a pet out of it. She went to the new bathroom and watched as they killed and buried it, unable to keep back the tears she wanted no one to see.

Emma loved embroidering pillow cases. She washed them by hand. They fluttered on the line to dry, starched and straight, snapping in the wind. They were sprinkled with water and wrapped to be ready to iron.

Sophie believed Grandma darned socks or crocheted a table scarf to be alone in her room. She didn't like commotion. When the brothers scuffled in the living room, or raced around, she picked up her needles and what not; not saying good night, she'd leave. She didn't ever stay up to eat popcorn or play checkers. Maybe she just wanted to put her teeth away which she habitually worked with her jaw to correct. Maybe she wanted them in their glass of water, where they were magnified and smiling.

★★★

"Sophie wants a doll, Sophie wants a doll," her brothers chanted after seeing where she had marked the Sears catalog with an old shoestring in anticipation of Christmas.

Maybe if she had a doll, Leota's mom would make clothes for it, and they all could play together. Sophie tried to be hopeful and optimistic, having understood that being kind and conciliatory opened the door more easily than if she sulked or pouted to get her way.

In the same vein, she tried to think of ways to help people. "She's so sweet," people would tell her mother as she fetched them another cup of coffee or obliged an old lady by sitting on her sloping, silky lap. It was nearly hopeless not to slide off.

"She always wears a smile," Mrs. Rodahl said.

Sophie might have been thinking bad thoughts, like the old lady had on an ugly dress. But she kept those inside. She preferred the laps of men; they were unlike the women who cooed and fussed over her, gathering her closer.

George, one of the men who worked under her dad, always winked at Sophie when she accompanied her father on trouble shoots. They met up on those nights they went to the warehouse to pick up the equipment they needed, perhaps a new transformer or fuses to repair the outage. She looked forward to those moments. She blushed and put her head down. As her father logged them in, she would wander over and George would pull her on his lap. "Mighty pretty girl you got here," he'd say to Ben.

After Grandma came, the family started having company over for coffee. There was always a chocolate pie or cinnamon rolls, something that took way more time to make than Dorothy had. People were prone to just drop in. Sophie was treated as a baby even when she was trusted to pour fresh, hot coffee into their cups. Sometimes the cups rattled in their saucers as the visitors held them up. Mrs. Weist poured coffee into her saucer to drink it.

The seasons passed slowly for Sophie in her fifth year. She wanted to go to school so very much. Come Christmas, the Sears and Roebuck catalog practically fell open to what her brothers wanted; they had opened and pored over it so many times. They wanted green army Jeeps "*to kill the dirty Japs*". They moved the old shoelace, no longer white, but an uneven gray, from the dolls' pages to their page.

The shoestring looked as if it may have come from her skates. Sophie was convinced because she could see the spots where it had hooked against the metal. She hadn't been able to find her skates in a long time, even though she'd hidden them from Doug and Matthew. She couldn't keep up with their shenanigans.

Sophie changed the catalogue back to her page and flattened it out pressing down hard with her hands so it opened automatically to her page too. She tore some of the binding and it opened easily to her place.

Marie wouldn't even look at the catalogue. Sophie thought she seemed stuck-up, but Marie only wanted to be sophisticated. Her hair was long and she curled it under into a pageboy. She tried different styles out in the mirror. She paused by each mirror to look at her reflection.

She shook her hair now and again in a showy way. She always touched her hair in the back. Sophie's hair only curled into tight little coils. Her hair was annoying, too stubborn and too curly to stay in ringlets, Sophie heard her mother say. She learned about herself from listening to others.

"If she were a boy I could cut it to the scalp." Dorothy said when she checked her for tics from the woods. If she found one, she lit a match and heated up a needle, piercing the tic. When the tic let go her scalp, blood smeared into her hair. Her mother rinsed it with vinegar after washing and scrubbing until it burned.

"Sophie smells like vinegar," the boys taunted.

Marie didn't like the catalog except to look for toys for the boys. You couldn't find a doll like hers in the catalogue. It would have been too expensive. Her doll had come to her as a gift from their grandmother long ago, because she was the first grandchild. Carol was expensive, and Sophie knew she'd never get a doll as beautiful as Carol, whose real hair was brushed or braided, arranged in ringlets, or pulled to the back of her neck if it were a special occasion. Her eyes were blue glass and moved toward you if you tilted her.

For bedtime, Carol was changed into a nightgown, and her toes stuck out, pink and glossy. She was then wrapped in a pink and white quilt Emma had made. Her eyes closed as if she were asleep if you lay her down. She slept with her head turned to the side just as Marie did, like a real girl, never on her stomach with a pillow between her legs as Sophie might have done if Marie were gone.

Sophie grew up knowing her sister came first, but didn't recognize how much she was favored. It seemed only natural. Sophie expected to be last in line, and she was. Her mother had conceded to a bare bulb in the corner of the bedroom. One night, the rain lightly spattered the window and a branch scratched back and forth in a light wind. Even with the light on, she felt afraid. She often thought fearfully of Mr. Weidisaari across the street. His light had already been moved to the corner and was doused. He was home tonight. There was no lock to the back door yet.

It had become Sophie's habit to sleep on the floor, even if Marie were away. She preferred not having to make the bed in the morning. She could never do it to Marie's satisfaction. She liked the flannel inside the sleeping bag. Sometimes she asked for the hot water bottle, something Marie wouldn't allow in the bed.

On an evening when Marie was away at a sleepover, Sophie struggled to pull the zipper as far up the side of the sleeping bag as it would go. The zipper had caught the leg of her pajamas. She backed it off and ran the zipper as quickly as she could past that spot. She felt along her leg for the tiny hole it had made in her pajamas and poked her finger through it. She knew that on wash day, they would mumble over it and wonder how it happened. It would be mended with a tiny patch.

She arranged her halved pillow, the one she kept rolled inside the bag. Its counterpart undisturbed on the bed was needed to plump up the middle of Marie's baby blue satin spread. Sophie could scrunch her half and make it fit exactly the way she wanted. As she lay on her back, her fingers fiddled with the tear in her pajama leg. The scratching on the window grew louder as the rain began to fall harder. She fell asleep with the bag as far up around her head as she could manage.

Sophie woke. She felt someone's presence. She stayed motionless. Carefully, slowly, someone was pulling the zipper of the sleeping bag down. After the zipper caught where her fingers had toyed with the tiny hole, a hand slipped across her stomach, inching its way toward the elastic of her waist band. She began to tremble

Sophie didn't cry out. She drew in one quick gasp, and placed her hand across the top of the stranger's which was being held very still against her stomach. It was soft and hairless, not like her father's at all.

"It's okay, Soph. It's me, Dougie."

"Dougie?"

"Shhh, don't say a word."

She pushed his hand flatter to her belly before she tried to pry the fingers away. Something sweet passed through her, an affection for Doug that made her breathe differently with fear, but also with love and the want for acceptance.

"I want to show you something, so you know."

He raised himself up and pulled his penis out the slit of his pajamas.

When had he grown so tall? But then he was already in the sixth grade.

"It's like what Daddy has that goes inside of mama."

The penis was swollen and purplish except on the end where it was darkly rimmed. The color of the tip was that of his other skin, a soft tan.

"Soph, you have a place like mama's." His hand moved from the shaft of his penis to the elastic of her bottoms. He slid it under and down so that his fingers reached her vagina. She opened her legs, and he slipped a finger into that moist spot, between the folds. Gently he moved his finger back and forth.

"You're so beautiful, Sophie. You don't know how beautiful. I watch you every day."

His penis was very near her hand. She touched it on the tip. It was wet and slippery, like her insides. She could see in the shadows that it was larger than before. "Like this," he said rubbing it up and down.

Sophie sat up and rubbed it as he had shown her. Doug took her hand and held it away briefly while he unzipped the sleeping bag. "It can go inside you, Sophie. I will put it in very slowly." His breathing was heavy. His voice was huskier than she'd heard before.

He snuggled in beside her and rubbed her again, this time spreading the lips more carefully before pushing a finger inside her.

"Dougie, you'll get in trouble."

"Just be real quiet and don't move. I'll do everything."

He entered her, arranging his penis with his hand, pushing in slowly, and then moving more quickly. She cried out. She pushed on his chest. She turned to her side and put her hands protectively where his penis had been. Something felt torn.

Doug slipped away and was back in his bed before their mother came to check. Sophie was working on the zipper. "Are you having bad dreams, again?"

"I'm cold," she said, shivering. Her mother brought the Navajo blanket.

She didn't sleep, but lay on her stomach, sacrificing her pillow to ease the ache where she felt inside out.

The following day, Sophie was sore, and the skin burned. Doug asked if she wanted to be pushed in the swing. He could push her highest of all.

"No, I have to read to Grandma."

Sophie often over heard her mother say to strangers that Sophie always caused trouble in the family. Sophie was usually to blame for what went wrong, at the bottom of it somehow.

She was eager to please, and often ran errands for the boys or Marie. If she got a Heath candy bar from Mr. McCollum, she shared it. A friend and retired cobbler, he lived in a trailer parked near the garage, and she visited him from time to time.

He was another ally, old like grandma. He rarely came out, but he watched out the window. Her father brought him groceries. Her mother did his laundry. Dorothy said he smelled musty.

Besides cobbling boots, he specialized in angel food cakes for their birthdays. It was always a Heath Bar she got if she visited him out of the blue. There wasn't much to talk about and she didn't stay very long. He was very formal and never hugged her.

"Stingy gut, stingy gut," the boys repeated at the possibility she wouldn't share. Soon enough, she shared, rather than bear their taunts. Mr. McCollum watched as she cracked the toffee in three pieces. They left her the smallest piece. It was hard to make them equal. Doug was oldest and got to choose first. Old McCollum shook his head.

She did cause trouble, she knew. Her mother often said, "Just run along. It's a nice day outside, and try to stay out of trouble."

Sophie heard the words so often, she believed she was what everyone said, just a trouble-maker.

"Go outside and play with the boys. Try to get along." her mother said if she hung around the kitchen coloring at the table.

She worked hard to stay between the lines. She was laughed at otherwise.

Her coloring books were full so sometimes she outlined everything in black which made her mistakes, where she'd crossed the line, less noticeable. The crayons were nubs, their papers rubbed off; she had sixteen colors that went into a tin can. They were only hers. Sometimes she had drawing paper.

"What's that supposed to be?" Matthew asked.

"It's a horse," she said, thinking they were truly interested.

"I've never seen a horse that looked like that," Doug said.

Sophie leaned forward and covered it with her body. The boys stood with their backs to the window.

"Stand out of my light," she said. "I can't see with you standing there."

"No wonder your horse looks like a cow," Matthew said.

Trouble erupted if she went into Marie's room to get something because it was Marie's domain, and she wanted to be alone. Living in close quarters with her brothers, especially during the many rainy days, there was bound to be trouble. Their toys were not to be touched by her grimy little hands.

"She's just in the way," the brothers told their mother or, "She's making trouble again. Do something Mom."

She sometimes played with the dominoes, making long matching trains or adding up the numbers of a whole stack. They knew how she added them up and would replace what she'd already counted. She liked the set of Reader's Digest condensed books her mother got through the mail, but she had finished them once again. She kept the green Webster's Dictionary close by. She liked the book about the TVA project and how farmers lost their land and how unfair it was. Her mother said it really happened. She made a picture of someone very angry and wrote, "I hate the Tennessee Valley Authority."

But mainly she caused trouble by her very presence whether she was reading or playing by herself. She never told, not even when she was the Indian tied to an alder tree while they threw pebbles at her. Matthew wasn't a good shot, and Doug aimed high. Nor did she tell when the boys began to slip pieces of lumber down to the lake.

Ben had reinforced to them all many times they were not to go on Mr. Weidisaari's property. The old man had been there long before Sophie was born.

Disobeying, they all, even Marie and Leota, went to that side of the creek, above the dam, an area shaded by evergreens, the black earth studded with sleek, chamois colored hemlock cones small and tight. With the light boring through, in cadence with the soughing of the trees, the spots moved lazily, especially late afternoon. After a deep sigh, your breath went away; it was like the sense of being in a cathedral, pristine and vibrant, when reverence came over you. An epiphany except that it happened not just once, but every time you came under the trees.

Because of the Hemlock, the old man had planted years before; none of the annoying brush grew beneath the trees. Sophie loved being there. Hushed, aware of grandness, she sensed a presence she felt no other place, not even when she'd answered an altar call.

There was a grayed barn planted in a large unmown meadow. Against its walls was where they picked blackberries in the summertime.

Inside the barn, the boys had discovered an unfinished boat which seemed more like a ship, though in retrospect it was probably another gill-netter like he already had. The boys crawled in and pretended to turn the wheel. They found an old net in his shed, rotted and reeking of dead fish. They spread it and tied on faded buoys that were cracked and mottled.

The barn would have to be dismantled in order to release the boat. Since Mr. Weidisaari seemed so old to them they wondered whether he would ever take it to the river. They wanted to see when he did it, eager for the spectacle of the barn coming down and the boat being launched into the Columbia.

The tilting building became a playhouse for the boys. They brought in weathered gray boards that lay around so they could walk across its breadth. They were pirates. They were giants like the ones Jack feared in the children's story of Jack and the Beanstalk. Sophie couldn't climb up. She wasn't allowed.

"You're Jack, Sophie. You be Jack. Just try to get up here. Fee, Fi, Fo, Fum. I smell the blood of an Englishman."

Mr. Weidisaari had dammed the creek, and the dam, about twelve feet high, was old, leaning back, like the headboard of a wide sleigh bed, and the blackened wood, like unpolished ebony, appeared weak and rotted with parts of it missing. Her brothers said it was the creosote that made it black.

Maybe there was creosote in the logs of his house as well, Sophie figured. The little cabin where he lived was black and hardly showed up at night. Sophie felt afraid of him. He was dark and wore a hat that shaded his face.

"There's no need to be scared, Sophie, he's an old man," Dorothy said.

Sophie looked at her grandmother, and she hunched her shoulders and brought her arms together as if she agreed with Sophie. What if Mr Weidisaari did what Dougie did that night? Sophie felt more afraid now than ever.

Sometimes her father got the go ahead from Mr. Weidisaari, and they built a campfire at the site of the dam. The pine would burn hot and quickly, throwing sparks into the night until it died down. Sophie didn't burn her Marshmallows; she liked them brown, not on fire like Doug and Matthew. Her way, you could slip one golden layer off at a time. Her father helped her cut the stick and hold them just above the embers.

Ben showed the boys how to put out the fire, so that it was absolutely safe when they left. Fire prevention was mandated. Smoky, the Bear, signs dotted the highways. Because the loggers were in the woods, the county put out warnings and some days Crown Zellerbach was shut down by the county. The men were idle. They couldn't cut or haul any timber out of the mountains.

The dam was a bother to her father's mind. "It's high time Mr. Weidisaari took down that dam," he said. "It will probably give way on its own here pretty soon."

Sophie never knew if he talked with Mr. Weidisaari about it or not.

Around the banks of the dammed creek was thick brush, embracing the hand-made barrier, maybe even holding it. Insects with transparent wings hovered over a welt of mud circling the lake. The sound of the black water trickling through the thickets and over the edge was constant. In the middle of the lake was a small collection of debris that moved in slow circular motion with the slack current.

Different levels in different seasons were delineated like scars on its dark, spongey, wooden face. The water level could change by however much snow melt there was on a sunny day.

On such a day, Marie and Leota crossed the creek on the flat protruding rocks that looked like stepping stones, a short distance upstream from the dam. Later, Marie was going to stay overnight at Leota's house. Leota slipped and gouged her knee. To ease the pain, Marie showed her how to pour handfuls of cold mountain water over it. Marie could be so kind, but for some reason Sophie was a bother to her.

Sophie looked on, aching to feel accepted. She was jealous of Leota. Next time Sophie would skin her knee and Marie could care for her and put the cold creek water over it. Sophie felt like she would do anything for Marie's love.

The water in the creek was clear and pure and seemed to sing as it slid around and under the rocks, unlike the small lake downstream formed by the dam. That water was nearly stagnant with a hazy scum around its edges. There was a bit of an odor near it like the water from a vase of old flowers.

Doug and Matthew stood with their hands on their hips looking out on the small black lake. A fish jumped, probably trying to get back to fresher water.

"I'll be. There are a lot of them out there today," Matthew said.

"Let's go dig for worms."

"No, let's build the raft first so we can get out into the deep part." Doug said. They didn't realize the lake was shallow.

Sophie listened as they planned. "We've still got left-over boards in the garage."

★★★

Abe shifted in his chair. "Did Doug ever hurt you again?"

"No, but he let me ride his bike and took me to the lake in the wagon. I rode on his shoulders to learn the paths in the woods."

"May I talk of my sister?"

Sophie felt as if her opportunities to talk were coming to an end. Marie was still a stronger uncomfortable presence. She began, and Abe took notes:

Marie was nine when she finished playing with Sophie. She didn't want a baby doll anymore, like the new born Sophie had been. Now Marie had Carol, the grown-up doll, given her by their grandmother.

Marie was given the responsibilities of an adult when Sophie, the fourth child, came along. She was enamored at first, having a real baby to play with. Her mother was glad to have Sophie taken off her hands.

Marie got a chair, climbed up, reached into the crib and learned to change her diapers. She learned how to hold her head so it wouldn't flop. She tipped the bottle just so when feeding her. Dorothy had nursed the others for a year. She didn't nurse Sophie. Marie had her little baby doll mostly to herself.

Sophie loved her sister, and later as a toddler didn't understand her absence and alienation. She cried in the mornings when she left for school. Until grandmother came, Sophie had no one with whom to talk. Her mother was always too busy to just talk or ask questions of. Sophie toddled around on her own most of the time. She liked climbing, and remembered being on top a large oak desk, its top rolled back.

But she was growing up into a toddler. Marie's new doll, Carol, was a teenager and much more interesting. Sophie began to understand she was a bother, mysteriously and innocently in everyone's way, even that of Marie, the first person with whom she had bonded. This was all before Grandma came to live with them, way back in time in Sophie's mind.

Dorothy who had had everything done for her as a child and teen found keeping up with a family of six hard, even though she worked at it routinely. The house was clean, swept and dusted every day.

Washington State was like a foreign country compared to Tennessee where Dorothy had grown up before going to her dad's in Kansas. Her dad in Kansas saw her as a little tart and didn't pay much attention to her except to get her trained to do something or to marry some upstart who could tolerate her feisty ways.

Now, married with four children, Dorothy hated the rain and hated the inevitable mud tracked into the front hallway. It only rained at night in Tennessee, she told them. "The sun came out every day."

Having her fourth child over the span of so few years had sapped her, and it was easy to let Marie entertain and take care of Sophie. Sophie preferred the arms of her sister. Sometimes she became unable to be reassured when her sister was away.

"You were never cuddly, not even as a baby," her mother later told her.

As an infant and baby Sophie preferred Marie or the lap of her father. At five, she could be of help to him; she began to spend more time with him outdoors building or fixing things. "In his heart he is a carpenter," his mother said.

There were already too many people in the kitchen Dorothy said over and again. Sophie found it hard to know just where to be. She tagged along behind her father.

Until she became too big for the creaky second hand buggy, Marie pushed it down the gravel driveway, onto the asphalt, driving it unevenly between the asphalt and the gravel shoulder, over sticks and stones, up and down the inclines of the narrow Elochoman Valley road.

Marie was allowed to go as far as the crossing of the log train down by the Grange Hall. Sometimes, along with Doug and Matthew, they waved at the steam engine train. The loggers in their shortened pants would lean out and whistle and swing one leg. Marie believed they whistled at her.

Years later, when the old growth timber was taken, the little black single gage engine sat outside the city museum for children to climb over. It's probably still there to this day.

During that time when Sophie was a baby, Marie still played with the boys in the woods; they laid a moss carpet and fashioned a make-shift crèche. Sophie was placed there like baby Jesus. Marie was mother Mary and wore a head scarf. She was tender toward baby Jesus, and carefully swaddled Jesus' stand in.

They invented many roles for Sophie, and she was moved around like a doll. They made her giggle by blowing on her tummy if she became upset.

When she began to crawl out of her crib at night, she was put beside Marie to sleep. Marie would jiggle her bottom until she slept. She would make a bottle during the night. It would always be Marie's room where she was tucked for the night because Marie could be responsible.

Often the buggy had twigs in it, or leaves. Sometimes it was left outside with Sophie in it on a misty day, and her toes would turn pink.

But, all too soon, she became a burden to Marie. Sometimes she was left behind on a particularly bumpy trail when Marie played house in the woods. She would cry with no one to hear, then she'd be cuddled and sung to. Sometimes Marie shook the buggy until she quieted. Her bottles were cold. She was cradled and bundled and conversely left alone. Eventually, she crawled out of the buggy, she was that big, and Marie refused to take her along anymore. "Don't be a tag-along."

Sophie had a favorite blanket in the buggy but she never got it back. Later, it was ruined by the cat when she had her litter.

Marie knew more than any of them. She read aloud to the three of them, and they were like Indians squatting around her. Later, Sophie loved Zane Grey's book *The Thundering Herd*. Even though the buffalos were slain for their hides, she liked that Tom and Milly got together. Love was true, she thought, and could overcome hardships in terrible places like the wild prairie.

They practiced their letters and multiplication tables with popcorn spilling all over. Dorothy put up with the mess to see them occupied.

In the summertime they stretched their bedtime out. They played after supper until dark. "Ollie, Ollie, Over," came the call as they threw the ball over the roof.

They sometimes played Old Maid without Sophie. Oh, how good it would have been to be included. Marie was the one who decided if Sophie could play or not.

Sophie stole the Old Maid and stuck her in the cedar chest. They were stumped when no one ended up with her. Once they had ransacked Sophie's trunk and found the card in the sleeve of a sweater, she was banned entirely.

"Doug said, "Why does she get to stay up so late? When we were her age we had to be in bed by seven."

They read about Laura in "*Little House on the Prairie.*" Their grandma, who had never learned to write because she was left-handed, gave them the books, one at a time. Grandma could read before her eyes started going, and she wanted everyone else to know how, that and the multiplication tables.

Laura Ingalls Wilder was so special. Marie took time and showed Sophie new words. Their own grandfather was born in what used to be Indian Territory just when the books were written.

Grandma yearned for the breadth of the scorched prairie like some yearn to see the unforgiving ocean crashing in from another continent. Both forbidding, they pull at your heart as home, but then there's no real definition for home, only fantasies and longing.

Later in life, home within yourself can be hard to find, especially if your memories about yourself are confused and toxic as they were for Sophie. Look and look, and you'll never find anything but a transient home in this lifetime.

They could all imagine the cowboys and Indians swooping down upon the new settlers after Grandma told her stories. It was like another world. The boys wished they could have lived back then. They pretended to kill Indians every day. Sophie often played the Indian, and she faked her death.

Sophie was telling Dougie no; she didn't want him to come, and she locked the door when Marie was away. She loved him and wanted him to like her, but she was afraid. "But, Sophie, I won't hurt you," He said one day while they lay on the green moss along one of the trails.

She was winded from running. She stretched her arms out spread eagle. As he took opportunity, she pushed Doug's hand away.

"I won't ask anymore, Soph, I promise."

Abe was patient and wrote notes about whether she was five or six as she talked. It seemed to him her earliest memories were the most important and the most potent. What had caused her to feel separated from her father?

★★★

That particular Christmas was one to remember in many ways. Over the years, Doug and Matthew had cut trails deep into the woods in several different directions. They worked on them often, removing branches, cutting back the briars or laying stone where the ground was soggy. They had found their father's compass and made signs pointing in each direction. They also named the paths they had cleared of stumps and fallen branches. Their job was to find the family Christmas tree. They went out to scout their trails for the perfect tree.

Because it was Southwest Washington, the edge of the forest they walked through was at first thick with underbrush past their ankles. If not for the paths the boys had tramped into the rich black soil, they wouldn't have been able to see a way through the bramble of blackberry briars, thistles, sword ferns or even through the thick of the trees. The first part, the entry, was the hardest to maintain.

Doug and Matthew stopped to eat the clover, pulling each perfect leaf from its stem, smiling and puckering. The salmon berries, so rich in color in the summer were hard green knots on the bushes.

Limping, Punky sniffed about and half-heartedly flushed birds from the huckleberry bushes. There was a sudden fluttering and rush of wings as the small birds abandoned the red berries and settled obscurely in the tall timber. Punky plopped down on the trail with his chin on his paw. The birds returned. He whimpered, but the boys didn't hear him.

The younger, Matthew, followed the older as they walked on the path they had marked as "Eagle Nest", going beyond the foyer of brush that hid the forest. Now the tips of the hemlock waved like flags, and the cedars' branches, swept by the breeze, were reminiscent of a royal court bowing and draping gracefully, nearly touching the ground. The floor of the forest was almost bare of brush. Sometimes skunk cabbage sprung up with huge shiny leaves in a wet spot.

Doug tucked into a hollow stump and pretended he was a king, using a stick for a scepter and woven twigs for a crown. The younger knelt, stretched his arms and offered both hands full of clover as an offering.

Again, Punky rested. He raised himself with effort when they whistled and hobbled toward them. They couldn't remember a time without Punky beside them. Since their birth he had been their companion, their scout, and their protector, constant in his attention to them.

Punky's habit was to wait in the drive to greet Ben when he came from work. True to daily ritual, he stopped in front of the boys, barked and turned away, heading home. When they called him, he sat momentarily in the path and looked back, as if deciding what to do. Then he barked twice and turned.

He left the boys to return to sit in the driveway, nose pointed toward the road. There he waited for the Public Utility District's line truck to pull in. It must have been about four o'clock by the time Ben arrived home. Punky could tell time, they always said. Sophie and Punky waited for the truck, the sound it made gearing down, the crunch on the gravel.

In the woods the boys came upon an occasional deciduous alder, bare leafed, its stark branches stiff and inflexible in the breeze. Springing up in the slightest shaft of sunlight, the alders were invasive and poached the light, but the young evergreen timber overtook them in time. Slim and leafless until spring, the alders provided the boys with its cones: strobilus, shaped like small lanterns that hang all winter.

As was their habit, the boys threw them at a nearby tree, listening for the sharp whack. The cones, one sure way to identify alders, could provide ammunition for an afternoon of target practice. Mathew's arm was shorter and not as strong, and he consistently aimed wide. But remembering their mission, they pushed on.

Their search hadn't proved fruitful. The boys went deeper into the woods. Leaving the underbrush that caught and tangled in their pant legs far behind, they walked under the canopy of the forest and way past the end of their Eagle Nest trail.

They came upon a spongy floor of moss expanding at least an acre. Wooded with evergreen, it was swept clean but for the fir cones and litter of broken branches, like a modern, wall to wall rug with jagged branches and stumps looking like ultra-modern furniture. The velvet carpet crept over the fallen trees the boys had to hoist themselves over in their quest for a Christmas tree.

Even an accomplished artist might struggle to capture the lush green tones in the breadth of the moss as it flowed like a riverbed as far as the boys could see. Encountering the unblemished soul of the forest, they stood for a moment, perceiving somewhere in their innocence that it was a privilege to come upon such mysterious beauty. There was a rhythm: tic, tic, tic, from the dripping trees of a recent rain.

The boys stopped to count the rings of a freshly blown down tree, and they knew by counting the rings that some were several hundreds of years old. They couldn't imagine a time so long ago. Their sense of history included stories of the Old West, cowboys and Indians, good guys, bad guys. They knew things like the flat tails of the beaver damming a nearby creek would have been used for hats in the olden days. They knew the settlers had worn them, as well as coonskins.

Ben could tell them of the days of horses and buggies, but they only knew firsthand about Fords and Chevrolets. There were war stories from Europe that seeped through, leaking into children's play, stirring their imaginations about fighting a war.

Ben had been called up, then deferred. A green army cot was folded away, and they used the blanket of the same military green for picnics. Sophie had been wrapped in it as a baby when the ground was wet and being baby Jesus made her cold.

If the brothers had lain down and looked up, they would have become happily dizzy as the trees wheeled in slow circles, but they hurried realizing that twilight was deepening.

The magic of the forest can play tricks on you about time. Sunsets over the valley could dally and saturate the sky, prolonging the day like the slow drawing of a velvet curtain. In a meadow, the colors could slowly stretch across that elongated sky into darkening tones of purple and orange. But deep into the forest, like a switch, the darkness came, quenching the light of the stars.

The darkness came abruptly, falling even as they walked circles among the new growth, which were the offspring of a large spruce or a towering

Douglas fir. They were looking for the straightest and most beautifully shaped Christmas tree.

"Let's find a baby tree for Sophie," Doug said.

"I know she would love making ornaments for it."

Doug offered to drag it until they decided they could get it on the way back. Sophie didn't get the tree, but she would have been so pleased.

The big tree the brothers found was about two miles east of home. It was much taller than they, just as they had wished. Small moving puddles of evening light still leaked through the canopy of trees.

Briefly, they played hop scotch on them. The sky closed in on them in less than a minute. Looking up from their feet on a moonless night, they went back to their task of chopping down the tree. They had remembered to bring a flashlight just as they had been taught. It flickered weakly as Matthew held it and Doug began to chop with the hatchet.

Like other trees they'd found, having been given this responsibility before, it lacked branches on one side. They came to an agreement that their father could most likely drill holes and attach new ones. He had done it before, and they could use lots of strands of silver tinsel to hide the remaining bare spots.

When they brought the tree home, Marie would get to do the tinsel, and she did it the best. Doug cut the rather gangly tree close to the ground in order to keep the longer branches at the bottom intact.

They imagined it all decorated after the light slid away. The sound of their hatchet cutting a wedge into one side of the tree was smothered, without echo, absorbed in the forest before the shocks could resound. Finally the tree thrashed and fell with a rush and a thump, a young spruce with strong limbs to hold ornaments. They knew to jump back.

In the seeming silence one could hear the whispering of the trees and the last harsh calls of a blue jay. At a quicker pace, the dripping of the trees combined into one sound. The rain came harder and straight to the ground. Their wool jackets felt heavier to them.

They dragged the tree, disturbing the pile of the rug-like moss. The black beetles beneath scurried to find the dark center of their universe. They appeared blacker in the descended night. Their lacquered backs caught the gleam of the flashlight. Looking down, it was if the earth were moving under their feet.

Deer came out to graze and peered at the boys. In the beam of the flash-light, a doe nipped at the leaves above her head. Somewhere close by would be a buck with antlers. Any other time they would have been excited to see a buck, and they would have stopped to hunt it. But there were not even shadows by then. The rain exaggerated the night and doused any remaining light. The sky was impenetrable.

The rain shower let up. The Christmas tree swept a new path behind them, but they didn't find their old path. So far their way home swerved and circled upon its self as they searched. The boys looked around as best they could in the darkness that enveloped them. Doug stopped and swallowed. He said, "Let's find the trees we marked."

They had known to mark their way after they broke away from Eagle Nest trail. They had slit and peeled away the bark of a few Cascara trees with their pocket knives, exposing the trunk, a shiny wet surface, cool and sticky to touch. They had carved arrows pointing home as they went. On their return, they expected to have at least some light of day. It would have been easy enough to find them.

They had piled up the stripped bark to collect later because they sold it in gunny bags after it dried. They were told it was used for heart medicine. With their earnings they had bought Sophie's Christmas present already. Otherwise, they chose funny books, comics with cops and robbers, super heroes like Superman. They weren't so interested in Archie and Veronica. Marie said they were a waste of money and that they just stacked up.

At home Punky had hopped alongside the truck to welcome Ben. As he removed his caulk boots, loosening and flicking aside their leather laces, Punky licked the thick waterproofed toes darkened with creosote. After the boots were pulled off, and as he was being petted and talked to, Punky slumped at the father's feet.

Punky was special, a good and faithful friend to the boys. If the boys were being whipped, Punky whined and walked in circles. If they threw a ball he brought it back and dropped it at their feet. He was rarely inside. Their mother didn't allow it. Sophie, Punky and her father sat together on the front stoop, waiting for the return of the boys. Punky's tail didn't wag as he lay there.

The boys were feeling their way in the dark; they embraced the trees and searched with their hands for the wet trunks of the cascara they had marked.

They scuffed with their feet to find the peeled bark beneath. They continued one direction and then another. The birds were quiet. They heard the "*who whoo*" of a spotted owl. The younger boy's shoulders hunched as he lifted the top of the tree.

They heard a rustle in the brush alongside them. Some creature slipped away, breaking branches, perhaps more deer or a bear, like ghosts in the forest. They were afraid because bears didn't always hibernate this early into winter. Matthew and Doug didn't know the habits of bears at night, and so they didn't speak out loud. They just whispered.

The boys' home and the acre it sat on were on the edge of the forest, and if not for the shiny leaved rhododendrons that bounded it, it would have seemed like an incidental meadow similar to the one that surrounded Mr. Weidisaari's barn. The virgin forest around their house had never before been logged. Never had a Caterpillar's wide tracks overrun the vegetation beneath the stand of evergreens.

The ground didn't have the telltale heaps and stump piles a gyppo logger would have left. Even a small dozer would have roughened the ground, and the scars would have remained for years to come.

The land was pristine, like nearly everything around them. Ben worked hard but he called their life in the Elochoman Valley the Life of Riley. Grandma said they had hard times back in Kansas growing up. They all should be grateful.

That night, lost in the dark, the younger stayed the tree's length behind his brother, stopping and starting when he did. They wore red plaid wool jackets though they may as well have been black, so deep the darkness had become. The wool became damp, but they were still warm inside. The rain had slackened. The sounds of the forest at night were new to them.

They tried turning the tree, but it wouldn't drag. Doug took over the finding of the trail home.

Their house where Ben waited, was like new, nearly finished, finally, with a cedar roof. Their father had split his own shingles. Sophie couldn't help except by staying out of the way as his axe came down. Later she stacked them. She admired all that he could do with his bare hands.

In contrast, the shingles on the outhouse soon to be dismantled were thin, gray and weathered. The privy seemed to have been there since time began. It stood somewhat crookedly behind the house. It had two holes, but no one ever used it with anyone else. For Punky's part, he walked with everyone who went to the outhouse out and back, even during the night.

Sometimes they threw rocks at it but Matthew couldn't hit the broad side of a barn. It was discovered the past summer he didn't have good eyes and from then on he had to wear glasses.

The third building was the pump house for the well Ben had dug. The shakes were still bright and wet looking, so recently had it been built. When digging the well, the boys had carried the passed-along buckets of wet red clay to dump on the edge of the property. An old white-bearded friend in bib overalls had dowsed with his L-shaped divining rod, and their first attempt at digging was a success. The boys handled the douser, smoothened by years of use. Sophie wanted to hold it but it was too late.

Sophie saw that the old witcher's teeth were missing. Sophie's two front teeth were loose, and it scared her to think about how she might look. He was frightening to look at.

No more hauling water for indoor use. It came right to the kitchen. Finally, Ben could build the pink tiled bathroom their mother had wanted for so long. After the water heater was installed there would be spigots for hot and cold in the kitchen and in the new bathtub.

As it was, since babies, they had bathed in a tin wash tub on the porch, cold in the wintertime, making them shiver and hurry. They barely fit anymore.

Marie wouldn't use anyone else's water so she was first. Sophie came after the boys. It seemed to Sophie there were a lot of advantages to being the oldest.

The boys began standing instead of sitting in the wash tub to scrub themselves. Doug poured water over Matthew's head to rinse him, and they laughed. Matthew couldn't reach to the top of his brother's head. It was a melee. Dorothy was glad to be done with all the play that went on having a bath on Saturday nights. "You're splashing everywhere," she said.

Everything around their home had come from almost nothing, except for the initial small investment in the rural acre of land that allowed for a deep and wide yard. They had begun with the shell of an old cabin that had a stone fireplace intact and the outhouse in back. Until the add-on, the boys had slept in bunk beds near their parents, Doug, on the bottom.

This was the only home they had known. But their mother yearned for another place. They had witnessed her crying at times, her face reflected in the dark window she faced when she washed the dishes. Dorothy seemed to Sophie as if she were not content most of the time.

In the yard, a cedar shake had been smoothed and became the seat of the swing that Ben hung on the giant cedar It cleared any of the tall branches when one of the brothers pushed the other into the sky of unfolding clouds, gray upon gray, gray upon white, gray upon blue.

Sophie loved to swing, and her brothers enjoyed making her go as high as possible. A swing is good even without someone to push. But, you can only pump yourself so high. She was always last, but she learned to wait, shuffling her loafers in the gravel. She loved to stand barefoot and pump to see the sky by looking down and not seeing anything except the sweeping arms of the tree upon which the swing hung.

To build the sidewalk of salvaged red brick stretching from the road to the door, the boys had carried the bricks in an old wheelbarrow bought second hand. Sometimes Ben would knock off the old used grout with his hammer, but for the most part, the bricks were left rough, speckled the color of an old setting hen. The walk was perfectly straight. Ben had worked on his knees pushing the fresh grout with his trowel.

Punky, had taken turns being with Ben, following the boys back and forth, panting, tongue dripping. Punky had gone intuitively to the garage and brought the father's leather gloves, but they weren't needed. The boys worked in harmony with their father, and there were few words among them. Sophie helped as best she could, picking out the best bricks with the least mortar and the most corners intact.

When Punky was struck by the orange, county dump truck as he followed the boys across the road, he landed in the ditch, the same ditch where the boys caught tadpoles in the small ponds of their palms, just where they checked and waited for the miracle of the tadpoles becoming little green frogs. The ditch was pink with Punky's blood as it swirled downstream. The driver had speeded on.

They had carried Punky to the kitchen, bleeding especially from his right side, and it was several weeks before he could lift himself up from the kitchen floor. Their mother had cried too as she held the water very near Punky's nose and made soothing noises. They sopped up his blood with the good white towels, and for several days until the blood was bleached out they all had to share the same towel. The nearest veterinarian was at least fifty miles away. Gas was too expensive and how could they run up a big bill? Punky now had three legs, the fourth having been amputated by the father.

Too painful to use, it still bled when he scraped the stub accidentally. The brothers had wiped their noses with their t-shirts, holding their trembling pet while Ben worked the hand saw through the bone. After that Punky was welcome in the house where he lay down and didn't eat well.

★★★

In the woods that night without Punky, the boys, wearing their hand-made worsted wool gloves and red plaid jackets were trying to find their way home. Their grandmother had attached the gloves to a cord so they wouldn't forget or lose them. They held the tree with bare hands now rather than wear the wet gloves.

On this particular evening when the boys were out after dark, Sophie and her father had gotten chilled and came in from the stoop. Ben kept changing the recline of his chair, the big chair that was only his. He would lean all the way back, then pull the back up straight. He pulled it forward. The leather scrunched against itself as he repositioned his easy chair over and again. He drummed his fingers against the leather armrest. He put down his newspaper and tilted his head toward the back door now and then over the course of an hour or more.

"They should be home with that tree."

Uncharacteristically he smoked several cigarettes one after the other. He listened for the shuffle they would make removing their boots and hats, wrestling out of their jackets. It was dark and no light edged through the blue draperies hanging in front of the new picture window. Sophie sat in the stillness, glad for her father's company.

Dorothy sat, making an afghan for the sofa. "They shouldn't be out there in the first place," she said.

Marie said as she passed through the kitchen, "We won't be able to decorate the tree tonight unless they get home soon."

Punky who had been stretched beside Sophie's feet began to pace, as did Ben, going into the kitchen to the back door, back to the living room. Punky whined at the door. One could hear the uneven clicking of his three paws on the black and white linoleum tiles Ben had laid in the kitchen. Otherwise, it was quiet. Finally, near the door, Punky barked. Because of Punky's injuries Ben had wanted to spare him from searching the woods. He put black tar on it. Punky stood still for it.

"Go find them. Good boy," Ben finally said lightly patting Punky's unwounded side as he opened the door. He stepped out into the moonless night and called their names knowing they couldn't hear him unless they were close enough to be safely on one of their own paths. Sophie yoo-hooed, hoping to hear a comforting answer.

The trails began as one but branched out in several directions after all the brush. The pieces of bark were attached to a post Ben had set in the ground with a hand held post-hole digger. He swept the flashlight over the edge of the forest catching the homemade signs. He remained standing in the cooling night as Punky went after the boys.

In the darkened woods, the boys found other cascara trees but not the ones they had skinned. They drew a circle, explored fifty steps out and back, in single file. They moved and drew another circle. Finally, they decided to stay put.

Beneath the hollow of a downed tree, they agreed to pray to be found. Nearly inside the rotted stump, Matthew knelt and prayed. Getting up off his knees he helped Doug build them a moss covered bed. They placed the Christmas tree near their heads as a kind of wall for protection.

When the younger of the two fell asleep, the older took off his jacket and placed it around his brother's legs. He kept the hatchet near. At daylight, he would know east from west. It was the Eagle Nest trail they needed to find. He too drifted into sleep with his arm around his brother.

When Punky found the boys, after sniffing up one path and down another, he stood for a moment, just looking on. Then he burrowed his way under the branches of the just-found Christmas tree. Panting, he pushed his nose into the face of the dozing older boy and whined in his ear. He was winded and wet with perspiration. Still he had run in his own fashion; now he lay down heavily next to the youngest who continued to sleep.

Doug embraced Punky and buried his face in the white fur around his neck. He stroked his nose. He let some time go by so the younger boy and the dog could rest before he roused them. He bound the dog's raw right stump with a knotted sleeve from his tee shirt. He took back his jacket, glad to have it.

They went single file, the older dragging the tree behind him, the younger following while attempting to lighten the load by lifting the top of the tree from the ground. They were led by their oldest friend, Punky, who hobbled home without stopping.

Their father stood at the head of the trail. They saw him by the brief red tip of his cigarette. Ben rewarded Punky with what was to be their supper, nearly a half pound of ground beef for spaghetti. Punky turned it down but he drank and drank.

Under the single bulb of the garage, Ben nailed together two pieces of a two-by-four and stood the tree which was slightly crooked. Taking it down, he tapered the bottom of the trunk in an effort to make it appear straight when it was placed upright in the stand. He drilled holes for the branches they cut from the lower part of the tree to insert them closer to the middle where it was most bare. Once inside, in grand display, the tree went in front of the new picture window.

Even though they had hurried the search up, it was now a handsome tree. The boys were into the boxes, pulling out the strings of colored lights, making sure they worked. They had to try them, one at a time until they found the one that prevented the whole string from lighting up.

They had a pattern to vary the colors so red wasn't beside red and green wasn't next to green. The younger one handed his brother each bulb to try. The wrinkled bows were lined up in a row of varying sizes, some predating their birth. Some of the glass ornaments had broken. They lined the good ones up by color. There were pinecones from eastern Washington. The tinsel was stretched to its full length on the rug ready to be hung. Mari would hang extra where the tree was still somewhat bare.

Marie said, "I can't hang the tinsel until everybody's out of the way. "

They turned the tree so they only saw the best side. Doug went under the tree trying to fix more lights. His lips were tight and his jaw clenched. He may have been angry and, or,disappointed in himself. Maybe he felt guilty for getting them lost. It was that kind of moment. He pulled Sophie's head toward him since she was kneeling there trying to help. He rubbed her hair with his face. She chirked up owing to his affection and attention.

Noticing the skinned knee, he touched her scab, he said, "You know Soph, if you stopped bothering it, it would heal faster."

145

Later on after Christmas, Sophie stopped picking at that particular sore, and it healed more quickly than her other sores.

Dorothy was stirring a batch of fudge. They were happy together. The hour was late. Punky settled beneath the tree alongside Sophie, and the boys had to move their game of war. Green soldiers had come with the jeeps. They moved their whole mess, as Dorothy called it. Sophie stroked Punky's fur. He was trembling. She felt the deep sigh of his last breath. She felt his nose. It was still cold. "Daddy, he stopped breathing."

His last dream may have been about the joys of Christmas. Each of them was probably in Punky's dreams. Most likely he was happy like they were that the tree was beautiful and that the drapes were opened so everyone going by could see the lights from outside. They were there all together, crying softly. Sophie almost felt she belonged, united in their grief, and that her brothers might stop tormenting her when they were apart from the others. But tender moments pass.

The boys dug his grave that night near the edge of the forest, south of the Eagle Nest trail, and the younger sniffled. They buried him with only the refreshed flashlight to see. Sophie wasn't allowed, but she watched from the window. Their shovels sliced into the moist soil almost silently. Ben pounded a cross made of left-over lumber into the ground. The Christmas lights from the picture window were reflected on the cross. They stood and the younger grabbed the pant leg of his father. The older turned his back and walked away. Sophie wanted to hug Doug, but he shrugged her off as he came through the kitchen.

There were more gifts to open. Sophie gave Emma a package of sweet pea seeds and a dishcloth she had taught her to make.

The hour was late, already into the next day. The trough of grief they were in because of Punky's death was less deep owing to their affection for each other.

★★★

Sophie continued, a little breathless after telling the story about her lost brothers.

Abe, the boys gave me a real pearl on a gold chain. They bought it with the money they earned peeling Cascara bark. I covered my face, amazed. No matter what, they loved me like a girl. It was proof. Mother put it away until I was old enough to wear it which turned out to be when I was thirteen. I often went to mother's jewelry box and pulled the pearl out of its box lined with satin. I dangled it and let it fall against my neck.

The pearl was a surprise to all of us. Doug and Matthew usually went into things together, but this was almost out of character. They gave our father new leather gloves, still stiff, unlike the darkened and flexible pair he used at work. They gave mother a new broom. The old one would come in handy in the garage. For Marie, they bought a new dress for Carol. They found it in the Dime Store on Main Street. They gave grandmother two balls of white wool yarn. 'Oh, for pity land's sake,' she said.

They opened their Jeeps, given them by Marie, and began playing war under the tree. She was so proud to give them; they had been purchased with her babysitting money. The living room was littered with wrapping paper, and mother said they had to clean it up before they went to war.

Their new bikes were in the garage to be presented on Christmas morning. I looked for a small pink one. I knew it would have been hidden with theirs behind the old tires and the inner tubes we used in the summer in the river. My brothers could manage the big tractor sized ones, but I could barely manage the small one. Even then, I didn't swim across in the water that would have been over my head because I was afraid if I wasn't touching bottom.

'May I wear my pearl tonight?' I said. The tiny white pearl was a sign to me that I almost belonged. No gift had been so precious.

I was given my only doll that Christmas from mother. Amosandra, named after the Amos 'n' Andy radio show, dubbed 'nigger baby' right off the bat by my brothers and mother. I didn't yet grasp the term or what it implied except that it seemed inferior because it was mine and very different from any other doll.

I'd been given a doll that represented my mother's prejudice owing to her youth in the South. I didn't understand the ambivalence of course. I don't think she expected me to like or take care of the doll.

To Mother, the 'coloreds' were inferior, just like me, I realize now. The curly hair, my awkwardness, my tendency to cause trouble … I guess it just made sense to her to give me what she thought was a lesser doll, a 'nigger baby' Though her opinion wasn't true, she held onto it. It was just natural to give me a 'nigger' baby.

'Her name is Amosandra,' I said after finding the name printed on the back of her neck.

The doll's brown eyes were brightly painted, the irises very large and white; she smiled broadly. She was chubby. She couldn't stand up, but then clearly she was an infant, never expected to be a princess like Carol, and never to be entered into play with Carol. She'd never be welcome at a tea party with Carol. She had one perfectly stitched yellow plaid sundress, Leota's mother made. Her little shoulders were the color of rich chocolate.

Amosandra came out of the box with only a diaper and a tiny bottle that bubbled when you turned it upside down. I didn't feed her milk very often because it just came out right away on the diaper, not real like at all. I took Matthew's worn blue and green plaid flannel shirt, cut it up and made a blanket. I put the sleeves and left overs in the burn barrel under the ashes.

The gift of Amosandra seemed natural at the time. But later, I was taken aback, to have been given my own doll. In some place inside myself, I didn't understand. Unexpectedly, I loved the doll immediately.

My mother always said I should have been a boy. "It would make things easier for everybody."

One day I found mustard in Amosandra's diaper. Shocked, I decided not to tell. Everyone but me seemed to believe the doll was inferior to Carol.

Making fun, my brothers would sing, *'Eeny meny miny mo, Catch a nigger by his toe.* . 'Amosandra even poos in her pants."

'Leave her alone,' I told them. It was important that I protect Amosandra.

'Leave her alone,' they mocked. It became their habit to repeat what I said in a mocking way.

If I weren't careful, Amosandra would end up in strange places: in the garage on the ladder, under the bed, on the top bunk of the beds where my brothers slept. I began hiding Amosandra so they couldn't find her.

Looking and looking, I couldn't find my skates to go roller skating in the Grange Hall. I loved to skate and had recently turned the key for the skates to fit my new size. The ruined skates showed up several months later, rusty and covered with mud in the pond in the backyard where the frogs' croaking interrupted the night. I didn't tell because I knew there wasn't any money for new ones. Mother said it was my fault I'd lost them.

'You have to take care of your things. You're too careless.' Mother always said when my things disappeared.

I determined I would never let anything happen to Amosandra."

★★★

Grandmother was called by her brother Jack. 'Long distance calling, long distance calling,' " the four of us shouted. The call was person to person, so it was even more important than any regular call.

As my father stood holding the receiver, we crowded around him, and Grandma came from her room, still wearing her apron. Doug turned over the three-minute egg timer.

Holding her hand over the receiver, she said to us, "'Jack wants to buy my ticket back home.' "

'It's where I want to be buried,' she said, wiping her hands on her apron almost as if she were wringing them. Looking toward my father, she said, 'Next to your father.' Father took the phone. His voice broke as he said, 'We'll send your sister your way.'

Grandma's husband had been a successful drayman, carrying other people's things from place to place. When he was hauling a short distance he took my father, his only son. Often he would give him the reins to the team of horses. He wasn't allowed to crack the whip while driving the team, but he practiced at home.

When Father was twelve, they bought a new team. He hauled the short distances with the old team who knew the routes. He learned responsibility. The leather strap with which he was whipped was put on a nail, not to be taken off again. He quit school.

The day we went to the train to send grandmother off, the depot was foggy and the fog didn't lift until after Grandma left. On the way, we were crowded in the back seat, and some of us were leaning forward. I put my hand through and touched Grandma's shoulder.

Doug and Matthew ran around the platform, and then leaned way out to see if the train was coming though the haze. When they spotted it, they ran to tell, but by then everyone could hear it hurtling toward us. And then the whistle blew again.

My brothers said they wouldn't miss Old Evil Eye, but when the time came they hugged her closely. Together, they carried her trunk. Marie and I stood close to grandmother. Mother didn't come because there were too many in the car already. The train would stand in the Portland station for a half an hour, then Grandma would travel days and nights to get home.

My father always cleared his throat when he was emotional or serious and wanted to say something. Above the hissing of the train, I heard him. I looked to see he had one arm around Grandma's shoulder, and his jaw was clenched. Grandma held a hanky to her downturned face.

'May Marie and I follow the boys and see where she's going to sleep?' I asked. Sure enough, when I looked back, my father's shoulders were shaking. The two of them, my grandmother and my father, stood alone together encircled by the arms of the other and said goodbye. Kansas was so far, and times were hard. Knowing it would be the last time, I wanted to run back and crowd between them. Instead I twirled around one of the poles, letting my skirt flair. My own tears scattered in the wind.

When the time came, she held my hand and left an opal ring in it, our birthstone. The days between our birthdays were only three, and it seemed like one big celebration with two cakes in three days.

Old McCollum didn't mind making two angel food cakes. One could tell he felt rather proud and useful. But everything would be so different now.

'It won't be the same, grandma; it won't ever be the same.' " I hopped up and down.

'Live every day like it's your last, Sophie. You can't let what happens in life cheat you out of your time here.'

'I don't understand what you mean.'

'Like I said, someday, you'll grow old.'

★★★

I had turned six. The day was cool but sunny. Since no one was watching, Doug and Matthew went onto Mr. Weidisaari's property. I followed behind them that day by way of the road instead of through the pasture. As I looked into the woods, I saw the makings of a raft. The boards were of new lumber of varying lengths. They had laid an old door upon them found in the barn, but they hadn't nailed it together.

'We're not supposed to be here,' I said.

'We need one more board, not a new board, but from off the pile in the garage.' Doug said.

Go get another board and you can have a ride," Matthew said.

I drug it behind me, and it sent little jolts through my body as it bumped against the asphalt. I wasn't supposed to be on the road. The end of the board was roughened when I brought it through the fence into that beautiful forbidden place. The boys eyed the board.

'Good job,' Matthew said.

'If you don't tell you can have a ride. Do you promise?'

'I promise.'

They found an old, blunted hammer and a saw in Mr. Weidisaari's wood shed. They sawed and cut the wood on the spot. They hurried in case he came in off the river to find them. Some of the nails were bent and they hammered sideways to get them in. The boards split a little, but they were intact.

Using the bicycle pump they pumped up two inner tubes from the tractor that they had used in the swimming hole last summer. For the leaks they found, they used a kit with patches and adhesive, lighting the adhesive on fire with a match and holding the patch against the rubber. They used the frayed rope they had found in Mr. Weidisaari's boathouse and bound the tubes to the bottom of the raft. When one of the knots came loose they tied it again.

Perhaps three feet wide by eight foot long with wide gaps between the boards beneath the door, they were sure the makeshift raft would do to fish in the middle of the slow moving pond where the fish jumped most often.

'Okay, climb on,' Matthew said to me, shoving it through the mud onto the lake.' You have your turn, and then go home where you belong.'

I stepped on the edge. The corner sank into the mud.

'No, dummy, you have to step toward the middle.'

Pushing me back, Doug jumped on. He landed in the middle, and the raft didn't sink. 'See, it's a matter of balance,' he said. 'Here, try again.' He took my elbow.

Little waves lapped against my shoes. Their boots were waterproofed, but I felt the water inside my shoe.

'I don't want to anymore,' I said.

The water moved so slowly that the bottom was muddy and stuck to their boots. They didn't wade very far until they climbed on. With sawed-off branches they maneuvered out, the slow brooding current from the creek taking them toward the dam.

'I'm going home to tell.' I felt a little sick to my stomach.

'You're breaking your promise. You had your chance,' Matthew said.

I ran home to tell. Out of breath, I didn't see mother right away; I didn't really want to break my promise. I felt compelled to find Amosandra. I needed to be sure she was safe. It made no sense. I was going to tell, but because I had hidden Amosandra so well, I couldn't find her right away, and it took some time to remember. Minutes had gone by. I fussed over Amosandra, feeding her the little pink bottle. I knew it was pretend but I wiped Amosandra's chin anyway. I patted her back. The urgency to tell was gone.

It was nearly quitting time for my father. I imagined the beating they would get, should he find them there. Should I break my promise? I thought of the tiny pearl, thinking it meant I was making ground with them. Someday I would win their full approval.

My father returned home. Supper was ready, and after dinner he and I would work together on the last wall of the garage. The studs were almost in. It was getting toward evening, and during October the sun wasted no time setting.

After I had finished feeding Amosandra, I plunked her right in the middle of the bed in Marie's room because Marie was gone for the night. Tonight I'll read, I thought. It was a romance novel, and I was learning about having a boyfriend and being kissed. Dougie hadn't kissed me. I separated what Dougie had done from romance. I hated disappointing Doug, but I had to for some reason.

★★★

Elochoman Valley
1949

Busy with their fishing poles, attaching the worms, Matthew and Doug didn't notice how close they were to the dam. The makeshift steering poles weren't touching bottom as they had expected.

An inner tube detached itself when one corner of the raft rammed and stuck against the weak timbered dike. The hole in the dam held the raft by one corner. Doug lay flat to retrieve the bobbing tube, trying to secure it. The raft pitched forward. Doug slipped into the water. Matthew had knelt, thinking to hold Doug while he stretched for the tube.

Doug tried to swim ashore; he gave a leaping jump to reach the bank, but his boots, filled to the calf with silt and water, pulled him under. He lay against the bank, his arms outstretched, his boots still in the mud, the toes of his boots caught on the slippery bank.

The raft jammed against the dam, held suddenly motionless at an odd angle causing Matthew to fall. Against the dark, rotted wood, the small home-made vessel looked brand new, as if it should have kept them safe. As the makeshift raft turned slowly over, knocking and splashing against the dam, one of Matthew's boots was trapped between the boards.

Only his hung up leg, muddied and useless, was visible. Though no one heard, there were three distinct splashes, almost as if a fish were teasing a line. There had to have been the splash of Doug slipping into the lake; another splash when the raft tipped over; then the sound of Matthew hitting the water nearly head first. He must have floundered briefly, sharp smacks against the water. The lake stilled. Evening crept in, as gently as ever; the breeze picked up as it sometimes does at twilight, rustling the higher branches, quieting the birds.

At home Dorothy said, 'Call your brothers for supper.'

Sophie didn't find them in the yard, but she called anyway. 'Time for supper. It's time to come home. Dinner's ready.'

The family had a special yoo-hoo that carried further. Sophie cupped her hands to her mouth and yoo-hooed toward the lake. She yoo-hooed toward their trails and toward the neighbors, but twice toward the lake, hoping they wouldn't get caught. She didn't hear a reassuring return yoo-hoo.

They didn't come storming through the door as they usually did, forgetting to take off their treasured boots. The heavy leather boots were handmade by their friend, the cobbler, who lived in the trailer beside their house. The boys favored them and wore their jeans cut to length like a logger would. In the meantime, Mr. McCollum was working on a new pair for Christmas. He was trying to judge how much they would grow. Little did he know their boots would contribute to their deaths.

Mother went out and called. 'Dinner time.'

'When did you see them last?'

'This afternoon.'

Sophie's father said, "Where did you see them?"

'At Mr. Weidisaari's.'

'Where at Mr. Weidisaari's?'

'At the dam,' Sophie broke her promise.

It may have been an eighth of a mile. They ran, Ben leading.

'My God, my God, my God,' he yelled.

Seeing Doug there and not seeing Matthew right away, Sophie began pulling on Dougie's arm to get him out of the mud. Her father took over, and she turned, seeing Matthew's leg jutting out from the water caught in the raft. Sophie screamed and fell to her knees.

After dragging Doug out further onto the bank, Ben left him to retrieve Matthew. Sophie screamed again. Dorothy clapped her hand against her mouth as they stood absorbing the scene she sees to this day. Dorothy pushed Sophie out of the way and knelt, sobbing over Doug on the land, turning him face up, slapping his cheeks.

'Wake up,' she said. Over and again, she slapped him. She turned him on his side. Brackish water came from his mouth. It seeped into the black dirt without a trace.

Matthew's leg was at an angle when he was dragged in. Sophie tried to fix it by pulling on his boot. Ben, in his wet wool shirt and bib overalls, pushed her back and turned them both over and began artificial respiration. He pushed down on one back, smashing Doug's lifeless face against the ground, then he leapt to Matthew, who lay there just as lifeless. Sophie held her arms around her own trembling shoulders. It was all she could do.

Her father wept. He leaned against a tree, his face in his arms. He pounded the tree with his fist, and the skin was raw and splintered.

'Ahh yiii, Ah yiii', came his cries.

Dorothy stayed on her knees with the boys. They had begun to mottle, their muddy faces dusky and gray.

Ben turned from the tree. Sophie hovered near his wet pant leg. 'Why didn't you tell someone?

He shook her shoulders; he spat on the ground, the anger spewing between his teeth.

'I promised, Daddy. I promised.'

★★★

Bayside Sanitarium, 1974

Several days passed in the telling. Abe was having trouble with the chronology because Sophie skipped from memory to memory, sometimes backing up to add a detail. Abe picked up early on the patterns of behavior among Sophie's family of origin.

Abe had little to say after the shock of Sophie's story. He turned and hid his tears although she saw them and heard them in his voice. He scanned his notes, front and back. He leaned back in his chair.

"I lost them and my father, too," she wept.

Reaching toward her, without touching her, Abe said, "How so?"

"We could never talk of it. I couldn't meet his eyes. He didn't ask me to join him to help with any of his projects. He seemed to have lost heart for them. We still played checkers, but the twinkle never came back to his eyes. He was gone from me. I was to blame for it all. I had no right to ask him to come back to me. I was guilty."

Sophie and her father had settled long before into a grave silence between them. The loss conducted an electric charge between them, posing the constant danger of separating them entirely and forever. They had never talked of that day of Matthew and Doug's death. It seemed the only way to survive. The distance between them was like the dark and deadly lake. They were spooked. It was a place they could not go.

Abe mulled over the side effects of a childhood lost to grief.

★★★

After the deaths Sophie removed herself from Marie's room without permission to Grandma's old bed. The door had a sliding lock.

"It needs airing," Dorothy said. "It smells of Witch Hazel."

Indeed it did. But Sophie welcomed the comforting smell. She wanted to be alone. She wanted to be reminded of her grandmother but nothing else. Marie said nothing. She moved her scarves into the bottom drawer and spread her clothes evenly across the bar in the closet. If Marie found something Sophie had forgotten, she left it neatly folded at Sophie's door. The house had stillness about it like the woods at the close of day.

The old dresser held her things from the cedar chest. The mattress had no box springs. She slept in the shape made by her grandmother, tucked in the sleeping bag she'd acquired as her own. Sometimes she traced the black lines of the exposed part of the mattress with her finger.

She hadn't shown anyone the ring. She tied it into a white Sunday sock and put it into the dresser until it fit her in seventh grade.

In her grandmother's old room, she would play the somber scene over in sequence leading up to the moment she had run home and hadn't told her mother, neither her father, even when he asked, "Where are the boys?" She had let everyone down, and her dreams were tormented, involving dark water and black mud. There was a corner of her closet where she went to hide. Sometimes she dragged the sleeping bag with her. Amosandra was already safely there, tucked securely with a blanket covering everything but her smiling face.

Sophie could go no further in her story to Abe. He didn't console Sophie as she wept, not in word or deed. An aide knocked gently on the conference room door and opened it slightly. She pointed to her watch. Abe understood it was time for another dose of Thorazine. He showed five fingers to the nurse.

Abe cut and pasted in his mind which parts pertained most to her healing. It was analogous to that boat Mr Weidisaari had built inside the barn. The barn would have to be dismantled to free it. Similarly, Sophie had some disassembling to do before she would be released from her torment. Emotionally, she had sat afraid in a closeted corner since the death of her brothers, nursing but never recovering from the wounds caused by the tragedy for which she was to blame.

To propel her forward she would have to touch bottom, that dark and dangerous place. She needed to be freed from the inebriation of guilt that can be replaced by sobriety and a hearty appetite for life.

Only she could retrain her mind to abstain from its gluttonous need for debilitating grief and guilt. The angels of her brothers weren't calling her. It was death itself; the idea of it had swelled in her imagination as a way to become perfect and absolved.

Abe knew when she wasn't distracted, her mind defaulted to guilt. If she were shown how to become conscious of this instinct and dispel it with logic, she could override the desire for it. Like a recovering alcoholic, she would learn to deny herself in order to be free.

He leaned back in his chair. She was ready to come off the Thorazine and transition to a more innocuous drug. She needed to be present and in the moment in order for the healing to occur. She needed her natural pattern of sleep.

★★★

1974

Ben was alone to on his way to see her. The night he got caught on the mountain was colder than he would admit to Sophie. The snow was coming at an angle onto the windshield and shaping itself around the pick-up, covering the side and back windows.

"Better stay put until the worst of this is over," the California Department of Transportation driver of the dozer said, settling his cap, dismounting from the warm cab. "We'll be back with a plough and dig you out by morning." Although Ben hadn't parked closely to the shoulder, the truck slanted to that side making it inconvenient to lie down. He had the truck because Dorothy had the car on her way to Marie's; besides the truck would be better in the snow and ice.

He was tall and the wretched, green army blanket he had brought along didn't reach his feet if he lay out across the sloping seat. Routinely, every twenty minutes or so, he started the motor and got out and brushed the truck down. He shoveled around the tires and the muffler. Thank goodness he had the truck and some tools with him.

Ben never quite warmed up when he ran the motor. The snow that he couldn't completely scuff from his feet piled around the accelerator, the clutch and the brakes, and began to puddle. The door scraped against the snow, and it was difficult to move the snow away so that he could open the door freely. He dug out, and the crunching of his shovel against the accumulated snow was the only sound in the vast field of misshapen rocks and trees.

He had known the forecast before he left Omak and had dressed warmly for it. Of course he hadn't known the plowman would stop him midway over Mount Shasta and request that he stay there. There were drifts and slides, he'd said.

He had unbidden time now to think about seeing Sophie, about how perhaps to help, to reckon himself to the situation. *Lost her mind? What did that mean, she lost her mind?*

His sense of responsibility for the boys' death had burdened his soul. He allowed the bedeviled memory as if it were a duty to do so; the memory like slow, crawling, slurry clogged his mind.

He was to blame for their deaths, the sole person to blame. What good to blame God or anyone, even old man Weidisaari's dam, when he himself was responsible for his sons whom he believed had been God's gifts to him.

Now, ashamed, guilty, Ben crouched over the steering wheel. Finally, he curled in the seat, the blanket wrapped around his feet. He had driven eight hundred miles and now he had to wait it out. Who's to say he couldn't have made it over the pass? He'd seen worse.

Ben woke to the truck being yanked from the bank, a sudden jerk, and then another more violent jolt. Finally, the truck began to creak and groan as it was pulled out of the drift. Ice fell away from the windshield, admitting a weak dawn. The sky was misty, nearly the color of the snow.

"You're a lucky man," the driver descending from the grader said. "If it hadn't been for that chain you pulled out there I never would have seen you were in that drift. When it caught the blade, I knew it was attached to something. "Let's get those windows de-iced and get you on your way. Are you good on water? How are you for gas?"

Ben pulled out a jerry can and funneled gas into the truck.

"Good reminder, thanks."

The chunks of ice flew away as he drove the rest of the grade, following a crew in a truck much like his own, looking for other victims of the storm. He helped drag out a man whose fingers and toes were frost bitten. The tips of his fingers were white and firm to touch.

One of the crew took his mug of coffee and added a bit of snow, cooling it to lukewarm. He held his blunt fingers in the mug and they began to turn pink. They took his shoes off carefully, then made sure he had fuel and water and painkillers before they moved on." Help is on the way," they told him.

Soon enough Ben was in the valley with clear roads. He had come pretty close to being in big trouble, he thought, in the ice box of his cab covered by a drift.

His thoughts continued. Although the water in the pond was shallow, the boys must have felt the pain of the cold before they died, and he hadn't before thought of the cold, just their struggle and panic.

He often wondered about those moments, those fractions of time while they were still conscious and unable to save themselves. How long were they afraid? Afraid for seconds or minutes?

As he drove through Redding and alongside Napa Valley on the east, he remembered how long it took before Sophie gave up the old sleeping bag. It was her hiding place when they couldn't find her. He turned the truck onto 280 toward San Francisco.

At first when he walked out in those woods to keep Matthew and Doug close to his heart, their trails would have been easy to maintain. But he couldn't lift a broken tree limb without howling into the hushed silence of the forest. Better to let the well-tramped trails go back to nature. He had thrown down the branch he held and stomped on it. The matted leaves absorbed the impact, and his sounds were muffled in the damp air.

Like that aging dam he should have smashed apart long before, he had varied and repetitious regrets that blackened and rotted but would not give way. Because of his long silence, he believed himself responsible for losing Sophie's companionship those years after the boys were gone. Now, their intimacy was forever gone.

It was if the little thing could read his mind. *God damn*, he thought, *she had a sweetness about her.* Her mother didn't seem to see it. As he drove the straight highway, Ben believed he was partly responsible for her undoing. Dorothy spoke of his change of attitude at the time.

He remembered the conversation with Dorothy: "I was jealous of you and Sophie. You shut out everybody else when you were with her," Dorothy said one night, leaning on an elbow looking at him directly.

"And now you're not?"

"There's something wrong between you now."

"I didn't believe I deserved such blind love and devotion. She lost her brothers because of me," he said. "You'd think *she* caused it."

Dorothy put her head in the crook of his arm. "She helped them build the raft. She was part of it too. I didn't see them go that last day. You're not fully responsible. We all are. It just happened. Remember Sophie helped carry the boards for that ridiculous raft."

There was more that Sophie needed, especially of him. After these many years, Ben intends to tell her how sorry he is that Matthew and Doug hadn't been controlled better and how he saw his responsibility to have disciplined them more often when they pestered and mimicked her. He should have known the children would be drawn to Mr. Weidisaari's lake. The losses were too profound to enumerate. All of it was his fault.

He thought of Sophie's attachment to Anna. Light-hearted and not given to moping or removing herself to brood, she brought Sophie out of her reading corner, rather out of herself really. They played together with the whole outdoors at their disposal.

He remembered her first visit. Even Marie found her refreshing. She was bigger than Sophie at the time, and Marie gave her skirts and sweaters that matched. Anna developed more quickly than Sophie. She was going to be a stunning woman, he could see. Sophie didn't have Marie's pretenses. She chose simple skirts and sweaters if she could get to choose at all.

When Anna starting coming almost daily, her constant energy was in stark contrast to his Sophie's. Sophie seldom spoke, and if she did, it was as if her voice had been buried with the boys. It wouldn't do to play horse and bounce Sophie on his knees anymore. When he pretended the horse was bucking her off, and let her fall between his knees, she didn't squeal or laugh as she had even a year ago. Something between them was lost.

Sophie was quick and loved learning, as was Anna and the topics they followed for a while at a time assured him they were good for each other. They spent time especially on how to care for and train horses. She always did love animals. They read about raising fainting goats.

Sophie still loved the outdoors, even though she was often indoors shut away in her room, so when Anna became a friend, they hiked and built forts out of branches just like the boys might have. Together, they pulled down the signs that marked the paths. Eagle Nest, the longest of the trails, and the others eventually filled in with fallen logs, branches and the natural debris of a forest the boys had tirelessly cleared. Sophie and Anna never went to the dam, even though Anna wanted to know where it happened.

After the boys died, Marie and Sophie didn't read in the evening anymore. They seldom popped corn. No one begged for sticky popcorn like before.

When it came time to get clothes ready for school, as always, Sophie was rarely part of choosing her own wardrobe. She hated hand-me-downs, but they were still good and should be used. "They're hardly worn," Dorothy told her, holding up a blue mohair sweater Sophie had envied before it had lost its fuzziness. He should have stepped in and seen to it that Sophie would get to choose her own things. Money wasn't as much a matter then. He was obsessed finding fault with himself on his way to Sophie. He ached for her to be little again.

Before long, Marie was off into her teen years, tracking well. Dorothy and she were strong supports to each other. Leota was always about, a sweet girl, but very quiet and sober. After the boys died, Marie wouldn't go into any part of the woods.

During high school, Marie came and went, and they barely saw her. Marie set her sights on another kind of life that the family couldn't provide. Dorothy completely agreed. She should marry well, and she should wait until college when there would be a better pick. She should shoot for a better life than she'd had. As the baby, Sophie already knew she wouldn't be supported through college, but she also knew she could, if she put her mind to it, find her own way through the four years of hard work.

Marie and Leota led cheers at the games; they marched in the band as majorettes, twirling their batons, lifting their knees high to the beat of the band as the small ensemble played John Phillip Souza's *Stars and Stripes Forever*. Leota's mother made all the short little outfits, even capes to wear between cheers if it got too cold.

Marie was given piano lessons. They bought a second-hand piano with an unmatched bench, and Sophie couldn't touch the keys, some of which had lost their ivories. It had to be on an inside wall to keep its tune, they learned. It took up most of the space in the living room, crowding the hallway to their bedrooms. Marie had a key and she locked it up and put all her music inside the piano bench. Sophie wouldn't have the knack, Dorothy said; she couldn't hold a tune

Marie said she would teach Sophie, but she didn't have a chance. Marie became pregnant. By then Sophie knew how you got babies.

Ronnie's car was red and souped-up. The chrome hub caps were like circling mirrors and spun slowly as Marie and he huddled together, his arm over her shoulder dragging Main Street on an at-home game night. Ronnie was out of school, but had stayed around after graduation and worked with his dad.

Marie left school. Leota's mother said Leota couldn't be friends anymore. Leota couldn't come spend the night. Marie who set such a bad example was unwanted in their home. Marie wept and said it wasn't fair. Dorothy was defensive and angry. The mothers never spoke again.

As adamant as Leota's mother was about the low standards Marie had set, she began making baby clothes and knitting blankets. She loved Marie, but Leota's future was more important. Leota threatened to run away, but instead she talked with Marie when they met secretly. Someday they would be best friends again.

The boy was nineteen. Ronnie Prestagard. He was disliked by Ben and Dorthy. He worked with his father on his fishing boat, and together they went to Alaska in the summers to catch salmon, which provided enough income for the year. In July when the baby was due, he was away. They called him in Juno, but the "*Carol Irene*" was still out. Their catch hadn't yet come in for that day.

When Ronnie learned of his newborn son, he got drunk in a tacky bar filled with locals. He called, slurring his words. Marie cried and told them all he would call the next day. He wasn't feeling well, she said.

Marie crooned over little Mike, but he wasn't soothed. Eventually Dorothy took over during the nights so Marie could sleep. Marie's breasts were uncomfortably engorged, the nipples crusted over and cracked. Mikey overwhelmed her, but he was hers. She was possessive and hovered dramatically. Dorothy called the doctor. He recommended cocoa butter for the nipples. They cracked nevertheless.

Sophie had no part in his care, except to help with washing diapers, folding them in triangles, the faint smell of *Purex* in the air. Still Mikey smiled at her. She peeked at him asleep while Marie rested. Being a mother didn't appeal to Sophie, but Mikey stole hearts, and hers was included.

Marie gave up nursing and began sterilizing bottles to feed him. He was eager, and began grinning widely after several weeks. Ben was besotted and took to feeding him. He could hush and soothe Mikey better than anyone. Grandfathering became his specialty, and in the years ahead he volunteered his help with fussy cranky babies.

Ronnie came home, but money was short, him being part of his father's crew and not having his own boat. He sold the hot red car and took a job as a cutter in the woods, working for Crown Zellerbach. Crown had housing for the loggers at the end of the valley where the men were picked up in crew buses and driven to the woods. In time, when the timber began to run out, some of the small, replicated houses went empty and fell into disrepair even though they were on skids and could have been moved elsewhere. The rent was cheap.

The camp was just five miles down the road, but Marie felt alone and out of her realm. Dorothy and Marie sewed curtains for all three rooms, but it was far from cheerful. The houses were close; one could hear arguing in the evenings and children playing in the unlit road late, without even the light of moon. There was no other baby fit to play with Mikey. Ben made up the difference.

Everyone but the women in the camp was gone by 6:30. The children had a long bus ride to school. They were the beginning and end of the line. The logging camp bus riders were known to throw things and fight in the back. As a student, Marie had been on the long bus rides with people she didn't know, like or want to be like.

Hating being there, among the loggers' wives Marie hwanted more. Her situation would change, especially if the catch in Alaska were good next year.

Things became better for Marie. Marie's father and Ronnie built a little home up in Rosedale away from the logging camp. There was a view of the river and extra bedrooms. Ben had invested in getting a rig, a brand new top-of-the line boat, and funded buying the inboard motor and extra cabin space. He wanted things to go well for Marie, but Ben was hell-bent on making Mikey's life good.

Mikey was always there in his mind, looking so much like Doug as a baby. Doug would be a man by now, he thought at the time. Surely now, they would be men of their own, good men. Here it was, Marie at thirty-five, planning a wedding for Mikey, who was too young but eager to marry his high school girlfriend.

Marie had turned into a good mother in those years. Her own wedding had been simple, and little Mikey had had all of the attention; toddling around as he was in the stage he went through, wanting to shake everyone's hand. He only cried at the wedding when he didn't get the first piece of cake. Dorothy had made it a nice wedding, somewhat awkward because there was a baby. As it was, Mikey was the center of attention and not the bride.

Now they called him Mike, but he was always Mikey to Ben. Later as a civil engineer he would do well. Angela, his high school girlfriend, made a stunning bride. She was nearly as tall as he, slim and fit. Together they loved hiking.

After Mr. Weidisaari's death, Ben had won the bid for the 120 acres across the road. He'd always wanted it but old Weidisaari hadn't wanted to sell it. The timing was such that he could invest his retirement money, and so he came to own the property where his boys had drowned, in mud more than water.

He ran 100 head of registered Polled Shorthorn on it. They were gentle, like pets, the color of red dirt. The prize bull ran free, and came to the gate when called. Since his mother was gone, he let go the milk cow and the chickens. That reduced the burden on Dorothy.

Ben missed his mother's hand churned butter, but it had been a hassle, the two of them not seeing eye-to-eye. Dorothy said it was one thing to be frugal and another to cause yourself so much work.

Sophie's father bought two horses, using the old cabin as a tack room. He left the old man's lanterns and potbellied stove. The old place began to smell of leather and saddle soap, and of that peculiarly sweet, pungent smell that horses exude.

Reggie, a gelding, may as well have been Anna's, while Sophie rode Amiga, the mare. Like everything they did, they read up, and the girls taught the Quarter Horses to jump. He could see how Sophie smiled, trotting back from a fallen timber she had leapt, keeping her balance, leaning forward and stroking the neck. Anna was good for her. So were the horses.

Sophie entered Amiga in the fair and took blue ribbons in her breed, and a purple in riding. She was a natural. To be truthful, her early life had been hard, compounded by the boys teasing and mocking her.

She'd seemed to be restored to a degree during those years, but the absence of her brothers was a hole in her heart no one could fill, not ever. However one tried to fill it, it was a pit, like a black hole in the sky. Sophie had nightmares, and Ben and Dorothy often went in to her and lugged her and the sleeping bag into their room.

Steve had told Ben very little so he had little to go on. He didn't know how ill she was or in what way she was disturbed. Perhaps it was an extreme reaction to the approaching death of Anna. Anna had filled a need in her.

Ben remembered pulling those ropy braids of Anna's. She displayed them like jewels, coveted possessions. He sometimes wanted to tear into them and release the hidden strands of blonde out of captivity.

"We've put Sophie in an institution this evening. Sophie kept talking about God, a Father, and messages she had received from Him. She talked of finally being accepted and forgiven by the Father. She mentioned she needed forgiveness for causing her brothers to die. None of it made any sense. She's been fasting and praying for four days.

"My mother insisted on a private hospital in Oakland where she'll get one-on-one care. We can put you up here after you see Sophie and get the gist of the situation."

The call had come the day after he had taken her to the hospital. Why Steve waited Ben couldn't figure. He spent the rest of the night putting snow tires on the truck, preparing for his trip over several mountain passes.

Maybe Steve's absence from morning until late evening had affected her for too long now. She was alone a good deal of time. Steve was all wrapped up in it, she'd told them, and making quite a name. But, Sophie had often been left behind by the boys as a child. Maybe she felt rejected by Steve. Maybe her studies, carrying the eighteen units and achieving the superior marks, had sapped her. She had a strong body. What now of her mind?

What had broken in Sophie just before the holidays? He wondered if she and Anna had ever talked over the boys' drowning. Surely Anna knew more than anyone how Sophie still grieved. Sophie wasn't as quiet with Anna as with Ben and Dorothy.

From that time of the tragedy, Ben remained more reserved in all he did and said. He stayed quiet, even with little Sophie who was always at his elbow, offering coffee or unlacing his boots. He still wore those boots Mac had made. Most comfortable shoes he'd ever worn. Sophie fetched what he needed: matches, his Camels, his Doublemint, and more coffee. He used Rolaids for the unrelenting acid in his stomach that crept into his throat.

Her little world was lonely, unbearably lonely with the boys gone. She tried hard to help others find comfort. She brought the afghan to her mother when she lay on the couch.

Like a bolt of lightning, Ben realized no one had thought to comfort her, least of all him, swamped as he was with his guilt. Ben believed in that moment as he drove that he was the one who should have consoled Sophie. Instead, he had been half-absent.

Yes, she wanted his company more than any other's. He saw now that she sought to be reconciled in spite of her guilt. Sophie had believed he was the mediator. His presence had seemed to pacify her, even though she spoke very little. He had never understood she carried the burden of guilt and separation.. Ben nodded to himself as he drove, and he saw that a window to understand her better had opened. This last idea, that he should have understood and comforted her more drove a nail into his heart.

★★★

Sophie heard the squeaking of her father's leather jacket, familiar and home-like and warming. She smelled the air of the outdoors even before he came to her bedside. Immediately, she opened her eyes to him, sitting up and shifting her scrubs. Ben reached for her.

She embraced him, pushing his shoulders away from her. "Daddy," she said. "Daddy, you're here."

Ben cleared his throat. She had known he did this when she was a child when he was about to say something of consequence or tell a story.

"A snow storm held me up or I would have been here yesterday."

He didn't tell her the full truth that Steve had waited to call or that he had suffered in the cold until dawn.

"Your mother is with Marie. Even though the wedding is not until February, you know how they fuss over every detail."

When Abe stepped back in, he saw Sophie's shoulders were relaxed. Abe smiled. She responded with a broad smile he'd not seen before. Given time would she know how to achieve rapport among her mind, body and spirit without the forceful presence of her father? She appeared more animated, less sluggish, and he left them alone. There would come a time when the three of them would talk. Ben and Sophie were loving to each other but formal.

The great food at the hospital had proved to be a hook back into normal life. The *"spread,"* as her father called it, had a lot to do with patients feeling like their needs were being met, that they were valuable and deserving of the effort and the quality, a significant factor for those imprisoned within the confines of their minds.

Ben noticed the tips of Sophie's fingers. "Can't you just file them a bit so they won't be so ragged?"

Sophie wondered if he had noticed her fingernails as a child. No one else had. She had bitten them, and they had stayed jagged until she knew Anna, that is, who had filed them and painted them a pale pink. She had picked off the polish, but Anna refreshed it. She had learned to have nice nails.

"We can't, Dad. They won't allow it."

Ben realized how confined and restricted she was.

Sophie had arranged for her father to buy the yellow dump truck for Sable's son.

"Now I know you're getting well. To a fault, you've always thought of others," Ben said.

She didn't know what he knew about her having gone insane. He did know her favorite truck was the yellow dump truck, which she played with alone beneath the big cedar among its gnarly roots.

As it came about, Ben was able to bring the yellow truck for Sable's son into the huge foyer that served the whole complex. He would keep it until Christmas Eve day when Sable was discharged, but he wanted to assure her that her wish had come true through Sophie's thoughtfulness.

"That's the very one," she whispered.

Sophie handled the small metal truck briefly. With both hands, she gave the truck to Sable. Her father watched as she ran toward the double doors to be let in. The truck seemed like hard evidence that her early memories had indicted her. It had been Dougie's, the one she played with whenever she could.

"I'll be here when you leave," her father said, turning to Sable. Sable was looking after Sophie, watching as Abe opened the door. Sable wondered what memory had been stirred to life. Why was she in tears?

Ben went to the payphone to see if he could visit Sophie. Abe would understand a moment had passed between them. He was one step closer to having Sophie back.

★★★

Steve, relieved not to be given permission to come, planned his day like an ordinary day, extending into the evening rally as usual. He'd yet to arrange for any special music or testimonies for the rally.

How could things ever be normal again between Sophie and him? Perhaps, after this ordeal, he would have a chance with another woman. The images of her out of her mind were branded in his brain, and the scar tissue would outlast the pain. Steve would never think of her the same. My God, when she ran down that freeway … He wanted nothing to do with someone who may be or had been possessed by Satan.

The doctrine had never been addressed in seminary. Speaking in tongues or the possibility of being possessed were peculiar to this new movement. He wasn't altogether comfortable.

He spoke with Alice about his concerns.

"It's a good job, Steve. You're being paid well and you're working directly beneath the senior pastor of a large growing congregation. Don't be hasty."

Alice said. "Besides, this pastor seems to be taking Sophie's breakdown into stride."

Steve knew the pastor treated him subtly different than previously. Even if the topography of her mind is not altered forever, Steve thought, I'll not forget those scenes. He was curious what the pastor would have to say after visiting her. Little did he know he believed she was filled with demons from hell.

In preparation for the evening service, Steve sought out the pianist, Lisa. She had moved to the alcove to practice on the organ, always used on Sunday mornings. She played "Amazing Grace."

She had swayed one direction to reach the stops. He noticed her slim waist and the way her buttocks sat pertly on the bench. "How sweet the sound," he sang. She turned her head, nodding, lifting her hand briefly to encourage him to continue. They sang together, a sweet duet that would have made many a mourner release pent-up tears.

Lisa stood. Her short skirt didn't slide well, and he noticed her thighs were fleshy in contrast to her torso. "I've heard what happened to Sophie," Lisa said. "How is she? But more importantly, how are you?"

She smoothed her hand down the length of his sleeve. "Why don't we do this song for the rally this evening?"

Steve cleared his throat. "She's awake now. She may be sicker than we know at this point."

"I'm so sorry. Sit down and we'll go through the song again. Our voices blend well. Did you have voice lessons in Seminary?

He sat. She put her right hand on his thigh. "Ready?"

After several times through, Lisa said, "You know any time you want to talk, you can call me." She pinched a corner from a yellowed piece of sheet music nearby and wrote her phone number.

He took the number. Later, he memorized it.

Lisa knew Sophie, but they weren't friends. Sophie rarely participated in the rallies and slipped away from the Sunday worship service through a side door.

Lisa was usually the pianist, but sometimes filled in for the elderly organist who had sat on the bench way past her time. Lisa sometimes had to adjust her timing when Sister Eleanor played in order not to be embarrassed. The song leader would have to turn and adjust the rhythm of her hands. Who could tell the old soul that her days of being an organist were up?

As they sat together on the organ bench, Steve flinched at the unexpected desire that coursed through his groin. He began sweating. He wiped both hands against his wool trousers.

By contrast, he thought, Sophie was not flirtatious. She slipped into bed easily when he returned home for the night. She might read until midnight or longer. He couldn't recall her enticing him with her hand.

It was he who initiated intimacy with Sophie. When she complied she did so wholeheartedly. He could hear her soft moan later in the bathroom as she pleased herself. He believed a woman should be satisfied by his movement and ejaculation inside her, but he was soon asleep after intercourse and didn't see it as overlooking her needs. They didn't talk of her not climaxing. Sophie didn't complain much about anything. Sophie was not his first but he'd not had many, celibate as he tried to be during his time studying theology.

That Sunday, as Steve and Lisa sang together in service, she held his belt as if she were frightened. He liked that she pretended to need him. She sang solo often, with confidence, smiling broadly. Her voice had great range, and she sometimes surprised the audience by changing keys. She didn't need him, she wanted him. They were a perfect match.

When Lisa accompanied herself she took more liberties and would spontaneously change the tempo and plead for sinners to *come home*. Often Shirley and she set the tone for the entire worship service. Lisa was no beginner at manipulation.

Steve lay awake that night. It was Lisa he pulled into his fantasies not his wife. He washed away the evidence of imagining Lisa, putting himself to sleep.

Alice cautioned him to cooperate in getting Sophie back to good health lest he seem uncaring to the church staff who asked each day. His job could be in jeopardy.

Sophie requested he not come until she had seen her father. He reported then to the church staff that progress was being made. In truth, he had not seen her.

Pastor, who had been rebuffed, didn't return, fearful of his own beliefs because he had not encountered real demons before nor did he want to. As much as he preached and blustered about *putting on the armor of God and having your loins girded with truth*, he was, in fact, afraid for himself.

Everyone was afraid of the madness that had descended on her out of nowhere. The drugged derelicts could be dismissed having come out of a scene of their own doing. But Sophie was one of them.

Sophie seemed to them an innocent. How vulnerable were they? Had they grabbed the devil by the tail by delving into spiritual combat as the pastor suggested? Some were spooked and returned to being Methodists.

Steve waited several weeks. Initially, she blamed herself that he didn't come. Finally she understood she couldn't go back, not without retreating into her old habit of incriminating herself. She could no longer feel submissive.

Sophie told her father of her feelings about Steve's intense drive to be successful. She couldn't go back, she said.

"I need your help adding on a carport to that new apartment," Ben said, without surprise.

They both knew she was past handing him nails. "Dad, if they still need someone in the bookstore down near the docks, I'll work there and help you in the evenings."

She smiled broadly, remembering herself as a child helping him in the evenings. "May I rent the new apartment? If it works out, I'll enroll in school there and work toward my Bachelor's."

Perhaps Steve didn't want to confront Sophie in Ben's presence. The man irked Steve. He exhaled strong character. He wore it like a badge. "Self-righteous son of a bitch," Steve thought.

Evidently her father didn't experience the dichotomy of the bent of his soul toward corruption as Steve did. Ben was not torn between good and evil. The daily struggle to be godly and Christ-like distracted Steve continuously, especially since he had become involved with Lisa while Sophie recuperated.

There would be a stigma surrounding Steve and Sophie in their current setting. The theory that the break had happened because of her failure to combat Satan's forces would leave questions in people's mind about Steve. His wife went mad, they'd say. According to the pastor she wouldn't comply when he confronted the demons possessing her. Steve believed he needed to separate from her, move on and begin another life in a new environment. He needed a divorce.

He also knew he would likely be pastor of a small congregation. Financially, it would be another struggle, a step backwards. A wife who played the piano and sang, like Lisa, would be a blessing. He would move up hopefully as an associate in a large congregation.

They were instantly attached, Lisa and Steve, both admitting later to an attraction before it was first expressed; i.e., when her hand stroked his leg. Without her music, he might never have been seduced.

Indeed, Lisa's music flowed, like the thunderous chords of a water fall or the trickle of a silver spring; sometimes it was sent from her hands with the rhythm of an ocean, tropical-like, music to sway to.

Lisa was fluent in evangelical music and could spontaneously change to a God-pleading, praise-inducing prayer of a song. With an old favorite, perhaps,

The Old Rugged Cross, she could summon the Holy Spirit to accompany a whispered altar call. She kept her head turned to perceive what would complete the spell. The pastor might nod, or the song-leader gesture to repeat the sweetness of a melody. She added several chords at the end of a song to give it a flourish, like a trickling stream of high notes punctuating the finish.

Finally, Steve came to the sanitarium. He brought Sophie's belongings. Her clothes, her shoes, her trinkets, all of it went into her father's truck. "I suppose you want this beat up trunk." She had expected his rejection. Their acknowledgment of an ending was mutual.

★★★

Abe saw, as he listened, the importance of Sophie's father's presence. As a child she had based her actions and opinions on his. She took on more personality when with him. Sophie had wanted to please him at any cost to herself. She had become a well-practiced actress. From Abe's point of view they both needed to acknowledge how guilt had deprived them of real living.

Their times together were pleasant but they didn't seem to really talk, not about times past nor of the future.

Ben talked of the beef cattle and how complex was the breeding to keep them registered, the timing on introducing Ike, the bull, when a cow was fresh.

"You should see him show off once he's inside the fence. He lopes and snorts." Ben laughed aloud as he described the scene.

"He'll never be the pet Hero was, just too much energy. He paws the ground when I snag the ring in his nose."

For the most part, with Sophie's permission, Abe was privy to their conversations. He listened for clues that would lead Sophie to re-access her sense of self. Spoken forgiveness was needed all around. Abe led them there, but they could not go. They shied away from pain.

Abe could sense he was trusted by Sophie and Ben. He believed something important might happen between them that would free them to relate less tenuously and that important communication of forgiveness would be key to Sophie's recovery. The dam would be broken and they would be released.

Dr. Savoire was persuaded to cut Sophie's dosage. He signed a release for two hours in the afternoons. Sophie was allowed out of the building with her father to visit Anna.

★★★

Anna's room was private, and she looked small in the bed cranked high for the nurses' convenience. She could no longer ambulate. The urine from her catheter was dark, tinged orange. From the doorway to the room, they could see the apparatus needed to keep her alive. Oxygen came from the wall behind her. The phlegm forming in her throat could be suctioned should Anna begin to choke. For convenience, the tube was roped over the IV pole, and it too hooked to the wall. Strands of clear tubing conveyed pain medication, fluids to support the function of the kidneys, dextrose, and a cloistered supply of lacking nutrients. Sophie's heart lurched. She took her father's arm and leaned her head into his shoulder.

As Sophie's father pulled the gray molded plastic chairs forward, Sophie began to sob into Anna's neck. "Forgive me, Anna. I've been very ill. I would have been here before now, but I had a breakdown. Anna, I went mad. I'm still in the sanitarium, but they're allowing me to come visit you along with my father. I can come every day now."

Anna took Sophie's face in her hands. She did nothing but fix her eyes on Sophie's brown pupils awash with tears. Anna took Sophie's shoulders and pushed her back, maintaining her gaze. Slowly Anna shook her head. "No crying, Sophie. I'm ready. Stay close, but don't keep me back."

Her voice was reedy and unlike Anna's strong, silky voice that Sophie loved. Anna's skin was like alabaster. The tiniest capillaries could be seen on her shoulders. The chords of her throat looked as if they had been sculpted to be emphasized by the artist. Arteries adhered and stretched beyond her neck. She looked regal, her head nearly bald but shining with new blonde curls. She could have been a bust, the nose a bit blunted like a Degas dancer. Her eyes were hollowed so they became prominent. As with any sculpted work, one wants to see its shape from every point of view.

From the side, Sophie saw the strong arches of her brow, faintly shaded with thin, white hair. The veins in her wrists, now bruised from the many times they had punctured her for IV access, looked to be blue silken chords. She was unrecognizable, noble seeming, an angel, shy to be seen below the sky.

Anna's breathing was slowed. She drew in her breath to say, "It's been a long time."

Her voice was raspy. She coughed slightly and her chest crackled as if she had pneumonia.

Anna had begun to withdraw several months before, but now she was refusing food. Sophie held a spoon of pureed carrots to her mouth and she turned her head away. Sophie offered the ice water. Again she turned away from the straw. Sophie bent the straw and offered it again. Her eyes flashed. "What made you sick, Sophie?"

"I wanted something from God. I just believed if I could be forgiven, you might be healed. If only I . ... Besides, Anna my brothers would be here today. They died because I didn't tell. I've never asked my father's forgiveness, let alone God's. Remember, no one was supposed to tell it was my fault."

The words spilled into Anna's heart, who, out of her withdrawn self, felt a gush of sorrow for Sophie. Sophie had been crippled all her life because of her terrible guilt. "But you were only six years old. Did no one tell you different?

"If anyone tells you they're special enough to God to be personal friends with God, they're fooling themselves. You're being called now to be yourself without the heavy load you've carried unnecessarily."

"Even so, I caused them to drown."

Anna sat straight up in the bed. As she reached for Sophie, she said, "No one has that kind of power, not children, not angels. No human being, least of all you as a six year old, caused them to drown.

Sophie's father went to the corridor. As he pounded his fist against the bare wall, it was if he were standing against the tree again smashing it with his bloodied fist as he had when he could not revive his boys. He wept against the green wall. He clenched his teeth not to cry out.

But he cried out as he went back in. "Sophie, no one ever thought to blame you. I am the guilty one. Sophie, tell me if a little child should carry such a burden. Don't let what happened keep you from living your life."

Their similar spirits had allowed them to hold fast to the false sanctuary of guilt and shame. He went to Sophie. They clung to each other. She forgave herself, as did he. There was no anchor of self-blame to keep them from going forward. He embraced her as he might have when she was five-years of age. They turned to Anna and she was gone.

Back at Bay Sanitarium, Abe walked the hallway, waiting for them to return.

The end

CPSIA information can be obtained
at www.ICGtesting.com
Printed in the USA
FSOW02n1913290118
43871FS